L E O N I E
G A N T

CURSE
THE
SOUL

The Harstone Legacy
Book 2

ISBN-13: 978-0-9943999-5-3

To Mike, Samuel and Nicholas

*a*s I passed the plain sign proclaiming 'Welcome to Walker Bay', I had to smile to myself. The last time I would have passed that sign, I was unconscious and locked in the trunk of a car after being kidnapped by two elderly witches. I was now returning to live in the same community with those witches. I was really hoping that the fact I was now moving my entire life to learn from and work with my kidnappers was really about coming home to a place I could finally truly belong, and not a severe case of Stockholm Syndrome.

After being kidnapped I had helped break a curse that had held my aunt prisoner and taken down a rogue witch intent on toppling my aunt from her position as coven leader. It wasn't often that a librarian finds herself in the middle of paranormal political intrigue and I found that I kind of enjoyed it, when I wasn't completely terrified and fighting for my life. According to Flora Harstone I was her great-niece. The current theory was that her nephew, Jasper, was the charmer who sneaked out of my mother's bed before she'd woken up from a one-night stand nine months before I entered the world. I wasn't saying that depending on the word of a witch was as accurate as a paternity test, but I was going to accept her statement on faith until proved other-wise. I had to admit that after a lifetime of living a nomadic lifestyle, the idea of settling into a community where I could belong was very appealing. I just needed to get used to the fact that I would be living in a town where it wasn't unusual for a centaur to be trotting down the main street. I could do that.

Five minutes outside the town limits my car decided yet again to test how far my optimism went. The wheel veered sharply and I struggled with it until I could safely pull onto the side of the road. After I managed to get my rapid breathing under control and peel my fingers from the steering wheel, I got out to find one of my tires had suddenly deflated thanks to a small piece of metal that was now embedded in it. If I believed in signs, and as a newly appren-ticed witch I probably should, this would not be a good one.

I couldn't help grumbling to myself as I went to the trunk and pulled out my spare tire, pausing to give the flat a good kick. It didn't help the situation, but it made me feel slightly better. As I was wrestling with the lug nuts, I heard the roar of an engine going past and then stopping. Footsteps crunched on the ground heading towards me and I warily stood up. On most days I would feel vulnerable having a large man in motorcycle leathers with tattoos snaking down his arms walking towards me on a quiet road, and today wasn't any different. I pulled myself up to my full height, which admittedly wasn't as impressive as I'd like it to be, while keeping a tight grip on the lug wrench.

"Can I help you?"

"Funny," the biker said. "That was pretty much what I was going to ask you. You look like you are in need of some assistance."

"I'm okay, thanks. It's just a flat tire. I've changed plenty before." Actually, I'd only changed one the day I got my license. My mother insisted that every woman should know how to change her own tire as life had taught her not to believe in the kindness of strangers. A lesson she was determined I should learn.

He stepped towards me, his hands held up. "It's okay. I'm perfectly safe."

"Sure, because nothing says safe like tattoos and bikie leathers." The words slipped out of my mouth before I was able to censor them.

The man's laugh was deep and rich. "Fair enough." He stepped back a bit and ran his hand through his hair, making it stick up a bit in a strangely endearing way. "Do you know Sheriff Tolan?"

I nodded. "I've met him."

"That's good. I'm his brother, Eamon."

Despite the new information, and that charming half smile of his, I still kept a tight grip on my lug wrench.

Eamon sighed and pulled out his phone. He held it out in front of him as he put it on speaker.

"Sheriff Tolan," barked a familiar voice.

"Hey, Conall, it's Eamon, just letting you know you're on speaker so watch what you say. I need you to do me a favor."

"No, I am not bailing you out of jail again."

I couldn't help the smile on my face at the pained expression that crossed Eamon's. If he was trying to prove his trustworthiness, he was failing miserably.

"I'm not in jail. I'm on the side of the road with...what's your name?"

"Sadie Goodwin."

"With a Sadie Goodwin, and she has a flat tire. I stopped to offer to help but she doesn't exactly trust me. I think she's about fifteen seconds away from swinging a lug wrench at my head."

Sheriff Tolan chuckled. "I'm sure that's a bit of an exaggeration."

"Trust me, I'm quite familiar with the expression on a woman's face before she's about to hurl a heavy object in my general direction."

"Miss Goodwin, despite all appearances to the contrary, my brother is trustworthy and capable of changing your tire. I would also like to remind you that unless there is a clear case of self-defense, hitting Eamon with a lug wrench would constitute an assault. I'd really prefer not to have to arrest you today." I could tell from the sheriff's tone that this was not something he wanted to deal with.

"I'll try to restrain myself."

"Thank you. Anything else, Eamon?"

Eamon smiled. "No, Conall, I'm pretty sure we're fine here." He hung up, slipped the phone back in his pocket and held out his hand.

I reluctantly handed over my lug wrench and watched as he deftly removed my tire and replaced it in far less time than it would have taken me. Before I knew it, I had my trusty lug wrench back in my hand.

I watched as he dusted off his jeans. "Thank you," I said, regretting the way I'd been with him earlier. "Despite the way I acted I do appreciate you helping me."

"No problem. I'd replace that tire pretty quick if I were you. The roads around here aren't really a priority for the Council. Flat tires are a pretty regular occurrence." He flashed me a devastating grin which I was pretty sure was his go-to weapon for all those women who ended up wanting to hurl heavy objects at him. "Maybe we'll run into each other in town at some point."

I gave him a non-committal shrug. At this point I wasn't

promising anyone that I would stay in Walker Bay for long. I was going to take this new adventure one day at a time. "Maybe."

"I look forward to seeing you then," he said as he walked back to his bike, roaring off in a cloud of dust.

I shoved my trusty lug wrench in the trunk and got back in the car, determined to recapture the feeling of peace that seemed to surround me when I drove into Walker Bay. I had never felt that way before. Part of it might be the magical wards that I had been told were in place around the town. Those wards kept non-magical people away from Walker Bay and the surrounding areas. They accomplished this by causing an overwhelming sense of dread and fear in normal people who ventured too close to the town. According to the witches who kidnapped me, the fact that I felt such peace in Walker Bay was proof of my magical heritage. I was still a little skeptical, but I was open to the possibility.

2

*W*hen I pulled up at my aunt's place, I was surprised to find Tilda Atwill waiting for me out the front of the house.

"Where's Flora?" I asked as I pulled myself out of the car.

"Something came up with the Town Council. Flora's been in a flap all day. She ran off about half an hour ago and asked me to show you to your place."

"My place?" I queried. "I thought I was staying here with Flora. You know, as her apprentice." I tried to quell the rising sense of panic. Had Flora changed her mind about teaching me the intricacies of witchcraft?

Tilda smiled gently as if she understood my fears. "You are still Flora's apprentice. She just feels that most relationships work better if everybody has their separate corners to go to at the end of the day. Your separate corner is not too far from here. A lot of witchcraft works better with quiet contemplation. As the coven leader, Flora's house is very rarely quiet."

"So, I get a house?" That sounded good. It was nice to know being the coven leader's niece had some perks.

Tilda grinned as she headed for my car. "Trust me, you'll be paying for it at some stage. You don't get anything in this town for free. Flora's a pretty savvy businesswoman, being family is not going to exclude you from that."

Well, that was disappointing.

Tilda's directions brought me to a small house that was a short distance from the bay. As I got out of the car, I noticed Tilda's apologetic expression.

"I know it's not much to look at, but it's furnished…" Her voice trailed off as I got a good look at the house.

"It'll be fine," I assured her. She was right. A real estate agent would have trouble coming up with a positive description for this place. The best I could provide on the spot was the phrase 'investor's dream'. It wasn't a quaint little cottage that screamed fairy tale, it looked like a house designed decades ago and never renovated since. Plain and serviceable. I felt the smile creeping across my face. "I like it," I said.

"If you're sure."

I could tell Tilda didn't quite get it. Part of me didn't either. If I was being honest, the house was kind of ugly, and not in an 'it has character' kind of ugly. I was talking straight up ugly.

Tilda looked over my shoulder as I opened up the trunk of the car. "Do you have movers coming with the rest of your stuff?"

"Nope, this is it," I grunted as I pulled the two large duffel bags out of the trunk.

"That's everything you own?" Tilda sounded doubtful. I couldn't help but grin. One of the benefits of my upbringing was my ability to live light. I always lived in furnished apartments and I could always move easily. I figured one day I'd settle down. I just hadn't reached that point yet.

"Well, that makes it easy. I figured I'd be helping you move in for the entire day."

"I aim to please," I said as I waited for her to unlock the door.

"A few of us cleaned it out so everything is set up for you to just settle in. The bed has even been made with fresh sheets." She paused before opening the door. "We'll help you fix up whatever needs doing. You're not alone in this."

"Just open the damn door. It can't possibly be as bad as you're making me think it is."

Tilda slowly opened the door and I got my first good look. Okay, not quite as bad as she was making me believe, but close. The furniture that was in there was a lot older than me and it showed.

"How much exactly am I going to have to pay?" I asked as I wondered whether the floorboards were safe to walk on.

"You can stay with me," Tilda offered.

"No, this will be fine." Flora was right. I would prefer to have my own space.

"Let's have a look upstairs," suggested Tilda.

I followed her up the staircase while noting that I might not want to run down them too quickly before determining how strong they were. She opened up the door and my breath caught. The bedroom was a decent size, but that wasn't what caught my eye. On one side of the room was a pair of glass doors that opened out onto a large rooftop deck over the garage. The deck looked out over the town and the bay.

I dropped my duffel bags in the middle of the floor. "It's perfect," I breathed.

Tilda laughed. "By no stretch of the imagination can you possibly say that this place is perfect."

"Can't you see the possibilities?" I asked her, my eyes still fixated on that view.

"Obviously not, but I'm not living here, you are, and if you think it's perfect, that's all that matters."

I did think it was perfect, and if I ended up staying in Walker Bay, I was going to have to work out a way to buy this house from Flora. There was no way I was walking away from that deck. Not willingly, at least.

"You hungry?" asked Tilda.

"Uh huh."

Tilda grabbed my arm and started dragging me away. "I know you're in love, but if we don't have anything to unpack, I think we need some food, and I need to bring you up on the latest gossip."

"It's been two weeks. How much could have possibly happened?"

Tilda gave me a look that was easy to interpret.

"You're right, that was a stupid question."

3

The diner was busy, but we were able to get a table against the back wall which made me very happy. Being able to watch the different types of paranormals that populated Walker Bay always filled me with a sense of wonder. Three weeks ago, I had no idea that any of these people existed, but as of today I was one of them. I had to suppress a grin when I saw Tilda bring out what I called her cone of silence stone. Somehow this tiny little pebble was imbued with the power to block other people from over-hearing our conversation. I had no idea how, but I loved it.

"How's Margot doing?" I asked. Margot was one of the two women who kidnapped me in the belief that I would be able to help my aunt. Unfortunately, we discovered that it was her twin sister, Isobel, who was the rogue witch who had cursed Flora, locking her mind in her body. When the curse had been broken and she tried to throw the curse a second time it had backfired. Now Isobel was the one locked inside a prison of her own making.

An expression of sadness crossed Tilda's face. "Margot's not coping very well. She spends most of her time at Isobel's bedside. She's pretty much withdrawn from the rest of the coven. Grandma's tried to talk to her but she's just shutting everyone out."

I decided to ask the unpopular question. "Was there any chance she was involved?"

Tilda shook her head adamantly. "Definitely not. There is no way that Margot was a part of what Isobel did."

"How can you be sure?" I persisted. "From what I understand, none of you would have suspected Isobel either."

"Isobel turning on us like that almost broke Flora. If we discover Margot was in on it too, it will destroy her and us. We don't have any reason to believe Margot knew anything about what Isobel was doing. Until we find out information to the contrary, we are operating on the belief that she is completely innocent.

"Okay." I guess it was harder for me to accept, but I had to remember that I barely knew this woman. Tilda had known her for her entire life.

We lapsed into silence until the food was delivered. Coming back to Walker Bay meant stepping back into the political intrigue that was swirling around the coven. As the new arrival I was going to need to be smart about what I said.

"Sheriff Tolan announced to the Town Council that he was a berserker."

I took a breath too quickly as I sipped my drink and choked. "He told them?"

"Huh." Tilda leaned back with a speculative gleam in her eye. "You see, I thought the important part of that news was that our sheriff, the werewolf who can't change into a wolf, was a berserker, a blood-thirsty fighting machine that hasn't been seen since the Middle Ages. But you seem to have glossed over that fact, as if you already knew, and you didn't tell me."

"Not my news to tell," I mumbled, trying desperately not to catch her eye.

"How could you possibly know about it?" she asked, her voice rising. "You were only here for a few days. I've known the sheriff my entire life and I had no idea."

"I'm observant," I said as I stuffed some food into my mouth to give me an excuse not to answer any more questions. I had promised Sheriff Tolan that I wouldn't tell anybody about the night he turned into a berserker and saved my life by tearing apart the golem that was choking me. It didn't matter to me that he had told the Council, I was going to honor that promise.

Tilda was still watching me and I kept right on eating, not stopping to allow her an opportunity to ask questions. Eventually she gave up.

"We're coming back to how you knew about this," she warned.

I managed to nod and shrug at the same time. Tilda seemed disgusted at my lack of willingness to share information. She waited for a couple of seconds, obviously hoping that I'd break and tell her everything. When I didn't, she decided to keep talking.

"Thanks to his news we're looking at possibly needing a new sheriff."

I finally put down the burger I had been stuffing into my face in an attempt to avoid any questions. "Why would Walker Bay need a new sheriff just because he's a berserker?"

"It isn't being a berserker that's a problem, although nobody knows how that is going to work. There hasn't been a berserker around for hundreds of years, at least not one that anyone knows about. No, the problem is that he's no longer part of the werewolf clan." She paused, obviously enjoying the fact that I was now the one desperate to hear her information.

"Why is that a problem?" I couldn't help the impatience in my voice, even though I knew she was relishing it.

Tilda put down her burger with a flourish and took her time wiping the grease from her hand with the napkin. I was going to need to tell her that this gloating and hoarding of information purely to torture me was not an attractive trait.

"In Walker Bay we elect our sheriff. Usually it's a pretty easy election because the werewolf clan will put forward their candidate and they get voted in. That's what happened with Sheriff Tolan, just like it has happened forever. The thing about the sheriff's position is that even though it's an elected position, the person who fills it has to be a member of one of the founding clans in town. It's a way of knowing they can deputize a number of people quickly and easily if things hit the fan. Werewolves are more intimidating and usually they are one of the largest communities in any paranormal town, so it just became common practice for a werewolf to become sheriff."

"So, what's the problem?"

"When Sheriff Tolan announced he was a berserker, he was outcast from the werewolf clan."

My jaw dropped open. "He's being discriminated against by werewolves?" I dropped the fries I had been about to eat in disgust. People sucked. Just when you thought you'd found a nice inclusive, community, it goes and shows you its dirty underbelly.

Tilda grimaced. "It's a little more complicated than that."

"They turfed him out because he's different to them. That sounds pretty uncomplicated."

Tilda rolled her eyes at my simplistic take on the matter. "Werewolf clans are built around hierarchy which is mostly based on strength. Strength is based on their physical characteristics and the ability to control their wolf side. Some werewolves are only able to turn during the full moon. The strongest can turn at other times, and the alpha can turn whenever he damn well pleases. In that hierarchy, a werewolf who can't turn at all is at the bottom with the children before their first turning. To be honest, he's probably below the kids, because it is assumed once they reach their teenage years they will be able to change."

"And now?"

"Legend has it that a berserker has the strength to destroy entire clans. He is more powerful than the strongest alpha. No clan is going to want a wildcard like that lurking around, especially considering the current alpha of the Walker Bay clan is his father, and the next one will probably be one of his brothers. Not to mention his relationship with most of his family has always been a little on the strained side." Tilda frowned. "It's all a big mess and nobody has a plan to do something about it. So now we have a sheriff who technically doesn't fulfill basic requirements." She sighed as she picked at her meal. "The worst part is the werewolves are looking to put forward another candidate for sheriff. We don't want that. We like Sheriff Tolan. He's fair, he's impartial, you're not going to get a free pass just because you're a werewolf."

"That used to happen?" I asked.

"Yeah," Tilda replied. "The clan hierarchy is a pretty difficult thing to fight against. Other werewolves that have taken the job of sheriff tended to be lenient on werewolves higher up the food chain. Sheriff Tolan has been different. He's just as likely to throw his father into jail as anyone else. Frankly, I think he'd enjoy it."

"And they're planning on getting rid of him," I muttered.

"Unfortunately, the rules are the rules. Without the clan backing him, he's vulnerable."

We continued to eat in silence.

"You two look like somebody's died. What's happened?"

Tilda's grandmother slipped into the booth next to her.

"Hello, Maude." I gave a tentative smile. "Tilda was just filling me in on some of the things that have been happening since I left."

Maude reached over and snagged a fry from Tilda's plate. "Yes, we're just a whirlpool of intrigue." She watched me carefully. "You seem less shocked than I was expecting."

"That would be because she already knew that Sheriff Tolan was a berserker." Tilda still seemed to be put out by that fact.

Maude raised an eyebrow. "That's surprising."

There was silence as I finished off my fries. I could feel the weight of Maude's gaze on me, but I refused to look up.

"She loves the house," Tilda said, looking for something to break through the tension.

"Really?" Maude seemed to be slightly shocked at that statement.

"That deck is amazing," I enthused, grateful at the change in conversation.

"That deck is a death trap. There is no way on Earth that you should step out onto it without a harness and sufficient health insurance."

"I'll work on it," I promised. "That place is going to look great once I've finished with it."

"You can do construction work?" Tilda asked.

"Well no, but I'm sure I can learn how."

Maude raised her eyes heavenward. "That statement has disaster written all over it."

I wasn't going to be put off. "I'm going to head back to the house and settle in. Could you let Flora know that I'll drop around to her place tomorrow."

Maude put a hand on my arm as I went to stand up. "Unfortunately, your presence is required tonight."

"For what?" asked Tilda.

"There's a special Council meeting regarding the sheriff situation, and Flora wants you there."

"Why?" I asked. I barely knew anything about the Council except for the fact that Flora was a part of it.

Maude shrugged. "I honestly have no idea. Maybe she's taking this whole apprenticeship thing really seriously and you are going to have to shadow her on everything that she does."

"Are you serious?" That did not sound like fun. I was beginning to think that I should have looked at the fine print before agreeing to become a coven leader's apprentice.

"Flora's never had an apprentice before. This is going to be a learning experience for everybody."

Well, that just sounded great.

*a*s I walked into the meeting hall, I almost felt like I was choking on the palpable tension that filled the building. People were gathered in small groups, whispering amongst themselves and throwing furtive glances at all the other groups who were doing the same thing.

"This is going to get ugly," muttered Maude, her eyes fixed on the stage at the front of the hall.

"And this is all because of the sheriff?" I wanted to be sure I clarified that point, because what was happening in this building seemed to be a severe overreaction.

The expression on Tilda's face as she nodded said it all.

"Let's sit over there." Maude indicated some seats that were on the edge of the aisle a few rows from the front. "We'll be able to move quickly if things get out of hand."

"Is that a possibility?" I asked Tilda, concerned at the way her eyes kept swinging from side to side as if we were in a war zone.

"Never can tell."

After we settled in our seats, I managed to have a good look around. The hall was quickly filling up and there seemed to be a wide variety of paranormal people. The centaurs stayed standing at the back of the hall, and I could see Doctor Collias watching proceedings with a keen eye.

"Well, well, well, if it isn't my favorite damsel in distress."

I knew that voice, I'd almost hit that voice with a lug wrench. "Hello," I said as I looked up at the sheriff's brother. There was an uncomfortable silence as we both waited for the other one to make the next move in the conversation.

"Didn't realize you were so involved in the community," he said.

"I could say the same for you."

"Guess we're both capable of surprises."

With that he turned and walked to the front of the hall. He stood beside the stage, his arms crossed as if daring anyone to question his right to be there. That man was truly strange and, considering my family doctor was a centaur, that was saying something.

"How do you know Eamon Tolan?" Tilda asked, her voice low and almost threatening.

"He changed my tire."

Tilda gripped my forearm so tightly I knew that there would be marks there in the morning. "By all that is sacred, please tell me that isn't a euphemism."

I shook her hand off and rubbed my arm. "On what planet would that be a euphemism?"

"He's a werewolf," she replied as if that would explain everything.

"I got a flat on the way here and he stopped to help. That was the extent of our interaction."

"Good, good." The glances she was throwing in Eamon's direction made me wonder about his reputation.

"Why is me knowing him such a problem?"

"Let's just say that avoiding Eamon Tolan is the smart move for any witch in this town."

There were times when I thought I was beginning to understand this new world I found myself in, but those times were generally in the minority. I could tell Tilda was a little on edge, so I thought a change in conversation was warranted.

"So how does this Town Council work? Are they voted in or are they appointed?"

Tilda visibly relaxed. "The Town Council is made up of five members who represent the founding five clans of Walker Bay. They are appointed by each group. You have Flora, she represents the witch coven. She's also the nominal representative of the other coven, although they would die before admitting it. Next is Aidan Tolan who is alpha of the werewolf clan and also Sheriff Tolan's father."

"The one who kicked him out and caused this mess."

Tilda smiled approvingly. "You have been listening. Yes, and let me just say that this situation is definitely in keeping with his personality."

"Don't think much of him, do you?"

"I think as little of him as possible," Tilda confirmed. "Next on the Council is Cary Heavyfoot of the dwarf nation."

"Cary?" I queried.

"His mom was a huge, obsessive fan of Cary Grant movies, so she named her son after him."

"Why not?" I murmured. That was no stranger than anything else that was happening.

"I think it's great," Tilda said, a little defensively. "The final two are Aliana Pantelis who represents the nymphs, and Dorota Bisek who is the leader of the giants."

I looked around the room. I was still a bit confused about how many paranormal races there were, but I was pretty sure that there were more than just five. "What about the rest. Don't they have representation?"

"Well yes, each race kind of pairs off with a certain representative. Dorota loosely represents orcs, trolls, ogres and goblins. Aliana has the satyrs and the centaurs. Sometimes the fairies and the pixies will go to her, but they're really not concerned about what happens with the rest of us. Flora is willing to represent anyone who has a grievance. Everyone knows not to go to the werewolves for help because they only help themselves. And Cary will grumble but he'll represent anyone who asks. The elves and vampires are more likely to go to him."

"There are vampires?" I felt my throat close over. Nobody mentioned vampires.

Tilda glanced over at me and I could see the sympathy. "Forget everything you've read about vampires. Most of it is untrue."

"You mean they don't drink blood?"

"Well yes, they do, but they don't need anywhere near as much as a lot of people think and they're really polite about it. Trust me when I say that most vampires started practicing affirmative consent way before the rest of the world did."

"But how…?"

My litany of questions was interrupted by a noise at the back of the hall. I watched as the Council members entered in what looked like a practiced procession. From Tilda's descriptions I was able to determine who was who. First came Aidan Tolan, his confident air similar to his son except that you could see that he had tipped over to arrogance. Following him was Flora in a long dress, her face serene except for the worried look she directed at me as she passed. Behind her was a beautiful woman, slight and delicate with a diaphanous dress that swirled around her. My guess was that she was Aliana Pantelis, the nymph. The only thing marring her perfection was the slight frown on her face. Next through the door was Cary Heavyfoot and he lived up to his name as he stomped down the aisle, his face almost completely hidden by the copious amounts of facial hair. I sucked in a breath when I saw the woman behind him. I know Tilda had told me that Dorota Bisek was a giant, but that in no way prepared me for the woman who ducked to walk through the door. Thankfully, the ceiling on the meeting hall was high and she was able to pull herself to her full height which I was sure topped ten feet. Her features were all in proportion with a normal sized woman, she was just huge.

The crowd watched as the five members of the Council strode towards the stage and took their seats behind a table. Next through the door was Sheriff Tolan, his back straight, looking forward. His eyes flickered as he passed me as if remembering that his changing into a berserker when I was attacked by a golem was the reason he was here. This was so unfair. He didn't deserve to have this happen to him. I'd only known Sheriff Tolan for a very short amount of time but there were certain things I did know about him. He was a good man and it looked like he'd destroyed his own life by saving mine.

Following him was Deputy Karl Iversen who I had met before. If there was any doubt where Karl's loyalties lay, the expression on his face destroyed them. I still had no idea what species of paranormal he was, but he could look scary when the situation warranted it. Obviously, he felt this situation applied. Sheriff Tolan also went up to the stage and sat down at the end of the table. Karl went and stood next to Eamon, his arms crossed, glaring at the crowd as if he held them personally responsible for this situation.

Dorota banged her fist on the table and the crowd quietened. "We are here to discuss the changed circumstances for Sheriff Tolan. The Council would like an explanation from the werewolf clan about the situation that has brought us here."

Aidan Tolan stood and faced the audience. "It has recently been discovered that Sheriff Tolan is a berserker. The werewolf clan will not tolerate such an abomination. As such he is now outcast from the werewolf clan. He is not welcome by us and he is not supported by us."

I leaned over to Tilda. "That's his father?"

Tilda nodded. "Fills your heart with joy to see the love, doesn't it?"

Flora placed both hands on the table and pushed herself up. "Sheriff Tolan has been the best sheriff in Walker Bay for decades. He has dedicated himself to this community and I say that he deserves to keep his position. More importantly, we deserve him as sheriff. The witches support Conall Tolan in his request to remain sheriff, despite the hysterical reaction of the werewolf clan to the revelation of his being a berserker."

Tilda winced. "Aidan's not going to like that one."

"You do not speak for all witches in this matter."

I craned my neck and searched the crowd. Up the front was a woman in a flowing dress and she looked angry. "The Path Coven agree with the werewolf clan that Sheriff Tolan is an abomination and shouldn't be permitted to keep his position."

"What the...?" I whispered.

"The other coven. That's Myra Hallybread. She's the daughter of one of the coven leaders." Tilda took a breath. "She hates Sheriff Tolan with a passion."

That was an understatement. The woman was almost breathing fire and she seemed to be drawing support from a small group of women with her.

"Who are those women behind her?" I whispered.

"The leaders of the other coven. They work as a triumvirate. The one who looks like she walked out of a bohemian fashion catalog is Myra's mother, Violet. The one with the really long brown hair is Ilsa Hocking, and the third one who always wears clothes that are so bright they sometimes hurt your eyes is Elspeth Pickering. Myra might be the one talking, but you can bet every word that comes out of her mouth started in their brains."

Flora didn't look angry at the intrusion, but I had a feeling that if there was a way to strike Myra Hallybread with lightning, she would have seriously considered the option. "That may be so, but it is the Walker Bay Coven that is recognized in this forum, and we support the sheriff."

She sat down to scattered applause from various members of the audience. Myra took her seat while focusing a venomous glare at the beleaguered sheriff.

Aliana Pantelis was the next to stand. "The rules are there to be followed. Sheriff Tolan no longer belongs to the werewolf clan, therefore he is no longer eligible to hold the office of sheriff."

Unlike with the werewolf clan and the other coven there was no heat in her words and no anger. There was simply a statement of the rules, and that made it devastating.

Cary Heavyfoot was the next to stand. "I believe that the value of having Sheriff Tolan as our chief law enforcement official outweighs the importance of him belonging to the werewolf clan. It is my opinion that he should be permitted to keep his position."

Dorota Bisek didn't bother standing. She didn't need to. Just sitting meant she was still taller than everyone standing anyway. "We keep him. The giants don't want anybody else."

Simple and to the point. I liked her.

"There is no vote on this subject!" bellowed Aidan Tolan as he jumped to his feet and I noticed quite a few people flinching. From the look on the older man's face I could see he was happy with that reaction. "The rules state that the sheriff must belong to one of the founding clans. He is outcast from the werewolf clan, so he is disqualified from being the sheriff." Aidan smiled grimly. It usually took me much longer to feel this kind of intense dislike for someone, but he'd managed it in less than an hour. "Until it can be confirmed by an election, the werewolf clan is willing to replace him with my son, Brian."

"Oh great," I heard Tilda whisper and looked over to see her rolling her eyes. "Just what we need, let's give the biggest bully in Walker Bay a badge. What could possibly go wrong with that?"

From the sound of the voices rising around us, it seemed that Tilda was not the only one with that opinion.

Sheriff Tolan surged to his feet as some of the crowd started pushing towards the stage.

"Stop." The power behind Flora's voice forced everyone back into their seats. Everyone except for Sheriff Tolan which I could see irritated his father no end. "Sheriff Tolan will be keeping his position as he is being adopted by the Walker Bay Coven, therefore he fulfills the requirement of belonging to one of the founding clans."

There was silence while everyone took in this new turn of events. People started whispering excitedly and I had a feeling this meeting was going to be talked about for days.

"No." The shout came from the front. It seemed Myra wasn't going to let this new development pass without challenging it. "You cannot adopt a berserker into your coven," seethed Myra, her face twisted with anger "He has no link to you, not through blood or family."

I couldn't believe how the council had turned on the sheriff. After everything he had done for them. As his future was being debated, Sheriff Tolan stood silent and stoic, staring straight ahead. Looking at him you would not be able to tell that his whole life was caving in.

My aunt smiled, and it wasn't a nice one. "That's where

you're wrong. This morning I consulted the Seer and discovered that Conall Tolan is the Destined Beloved for my niece Sadie Goodwin.

"Destined Beloved?" I murmured out of the side of my mouth.

"Soul mate," replied Tilda, her stunned expression telling me that she had not been expecting this.

Okay. I didn't know that was part of the plan. I glanced over at the sheriff to find the same look of shock on his face that I'm guessing was on mine. Our eyes met, and in that moment a heat rushed through me that I couldn't explain. I looked away from him before I was consumed by it.

"Are you okay?" whispered Tilda as she glared at other members of the crowd who were openly gawking at me.

"I don't think I like this plan," I said through gritted teeth as every part of my body urged me to go to the man who I knew was still watching me. I didn't know what Flora had done to me to cause this, but she and I were going to have words…loud, argumentative words.

Aidan Tolan surged to his feet. "That is not possible. You're lying."

Flora straightened and the hall became silent. Despite her petite stature every eye was looking at her and you could feel an energy swirling around her. "Are you questioning the Seer?" she asked quietly.

I had to give the man credit. He stood his ground and didn't bow to the power that was now clearly on show. I guess that was why he was the alpha. If I'd ever had any questions in my mind as to why Flora was chosen to be the coven leader, they were now put to rest. "If you wish to confirm my statement you are entitled to do so. I'm sure the Seer would be more than willing to grant you an audience."

An expression of distaste crossed the werewolf alpha's face. "No, of course not. I accept the prophecy of the Seer."

Dorota banged her fist on the table. "Sheriff Tolan is now a member of the Walker Bay Coven and as such retains his position as sheriff." A small smile flitted across her face. "Good luck with your new future, Conall, I have a feeling you're going to need it."

t was a somber group that walked into Flora's house that evening. Maude had stayed at the meeting hall to put out the numerous fires caused by Flora's adoption of a berserker werewolf. Strangely enough, some members of the coven were a little concerned by the unprecedented turn of events.

"That was interesting," said Tilda in a masterstroke of understatement as we entered the house.

On the way back I had managed to convince myself that this was all some inspired piece of theater engineered by Flora to save Sheriff Tolan, and I was going to hold on to that belief with everything I had.

"When did you come up with this idea?" I asked as I refused to acknowledge the sheriff who was leaning against a wall, his hooded gaze trained on me. "I mean, it obviously worked, but all you've managed to do is buy us a little time. It's not like we could keep this ruse up forever."

I went to get myself a drink, my mind flying through the events of the evening. Sheriff Tolan was safe, he was going to keep his position, and everything could go back to normal, or as normal as Walker Bay allowed it to be. After I filled my glass with water I turned around and leaned back against the sink.

"What's wrong?" I asked as I surveyed the group. Flora looked mildly concerned as she watched me. Tilda and Karl sported identical pale faces. I couldn't even begin to interpret the expression on the sheriff's face.

"You're all looking at me strangely. I thought this was good news. We just need to finesse the details."

Tilda pulled out a chair and sat down, her hands clasped in front of her on the table as she leaned forward. "Did you understand any of what just happened?"

I sat down opposite her. "Of course, I did. Sheriff Tolan is now in our coven, so that gives him a level of protection against instant dismissal and being targeted by anyone."

Tilda sighed and looked up at Karl who sat down next to her. "Do you understand what Flora said about you being the sheriff's Destined Beloved?" he asked.

I smiled and patted his hand. "We obviously needed a reason for him to be attached to the coven and this one seemed to work." I looked around expectantly. "How long do we need to keep up the whole 'Destined Beloved' idea? And how is that a thing, anyway?"

Silence greeted my query.

"Sadie," my aunt said patiently, as if explaining something to a child, "It isn't a joke and it's not a ruse to get Conall in the coven. If the Seer says he's your Destined Beloved, then that's what he is."

My mouth suddenly felt dry and I took a sip of water. "What does that mean?"

"It means you're mine." Sheriff Tolan's guttural voice shocked us all.

"Oh, this can't be good," murmured Karl. He stood up and

placed himself between the two of us as the sheriff stepped towards me.

"You don't want to do this," I heard him whisper. "Not here, not now."

"No," I said calmly.

Everyone stopped and stared at me.

Tilda broke the silence first. "What do you mean?"

I cleared my throat and stared directly into the sheriff's eyes. I wanted him to hear what I was saying. "I mean that I do not care what you or this town believes. My future is not going to be dictated by you or some random Seer." The sheriff opened his mouth, but I put a hand up to stop him. "As far as anyone outside this room is concerned, I am happy to play the part of Destined Beloved, or whatever this is to ensure that you stay in the coven and keep your position as our sheriff." I paused wanting to make sure that everyone was listening. "But I am just now getting my head around what this town is and who I might be. I do not have to believe in it."

Karl shook his head. "So not good."

There was silence as everybody seemed to absorb what I had just said. Sheriff Tolan studied me carefully, nodded once and left the room, Karl trailing behind him.

"That went well," Flora stated. "You could have been a bit more sensitive to his feelings. He's probably just as floored by all this as you are."

"At least he knew what a Destined Beloved is. Seriously, how is that a thing? It sounds ridiculous."

"A Destined Beloved is one of the rarest prophecies that a Seer can make. It is a cause for celebration."

"I'm sure it is when it isn't being used for political maneuvering."

Flora had the grace to look slightly guilty at my statement. "You're right. I was hoping for some guidance when I went to visit the Seer. I did not expect that to be her prophecy but when it was, I knew it would help us." She grasped my hand and forced me to look in her eyes. "I was not planning to use it unless there was no other way. I hoped Aidan would see reason, or at least have some paternal feelings for his son. That hope was misplaced. I want you to believe I wouldn't have used the information I had unless the situation was dire."

There was silence between us. I hoped she was telling me the truth. I had a thought and gave a humorless laugh.

"What is it?" asked Flora.

"I'm just remembering that you were the one who told me never to get involved with a werewolf."

$\mathcal{B}$y the time dawn was spreading across the horizon I had long ago given up on trying to sleep. Bundled up tightly against the cold, I walked to my normal bench in the park that overlooked the bay and watch the sun come up. While I'd been packing up my life over the last two weeks, I had not been able to shake a feeling of tension, as if I needed to be somewhere else. As that tension flowed out of me, I knew I had come back to where I belonged.

"Sleep well?"

"Really? You couldn't give me one morning where I was left alone."

Karl smiled down at me. "It's not my fault you're regular as clockwork. Why do you get up so early every morning? It's a bit weird."

Sure, I was the weird one. I noticed what he had in his hand. "Did you bring me a coffee?"

He looked slightly embarrassed. "Sorry, I didn't know you liked coffee." He held out his own cup. "You can have mine."

I shook my head. "You're right. I don't really drink coffee. For future reference I'm pretty partial to a hot chocolate."

"Noted." He looked pensively out across the bay. "How are you doing this morning?" He waved his hand around. "You know, after everything that happened last night."

I mimicked his waving hand. "You mean the Destined Beloved thing?"

"Yeah."

"Are you asking for your boss, because I would have thought he'd do the asking himself."

Karl sipped his coffee. "We had a discussion and it was felt that it would be better for me to approach you, less chance of an assault conviction on your record that way."

"So, let me get this straight, Walker Bay is so crime-free that you and the sheriff have time to debate who will interrupt my morning meditation session."

Karl smirked. "Meditation, is that what we're calling it?"

"It was either that or yoga, and yoga would have required me to actually move, so meditation it is."

"Seriously, he was going to meet you here and I thought that it would be better if I checked to see if you wanted to do him bodily harm."

I couldn't help the sigh that came out of me. "It's no more his fault than mine. I just don't know what everyone expects of me. This isn't my normal."

Karl smiled at the frustration in my voice. "You think this is normal for everyone? Destined Beloveds are rare. I've never heard of one for an ogre, not in all our history."

"Is that what you are?" I asked tentatively.

"Of course I'm an ogre. What did you think I was?"

I shrugged helplessly. "I had no idea. I've been trying to work it out for weeks."

"You mean that we have interacted repeatedly, and you had no idea what species I was?"

I kept my head down and shook it, only raising it as Karl started laughing.

"Thank you, I needed a laugh. You are the most polite person I have ever met. Why have you not asked?"

"It hasn't been easy. I just didn't want to say anything and possibly offend you."

"Do I look like someone who is easily offended?"

I smiled. "No, but if I guessed wrong you look like someone who could rip my arms off. I figured discretion was the better part of valor."

Karl smiled gently at me. "I forget that this has all been a shock to you. Yes, I am an ogre. Have been my entire life."

I tipped my head to the side. "I wouldn't have picked you for an ogre."

"Why not?"

"You're way better looking than I imagined an ogre would be."

"Are you coming on to me?"

"Of course not." I had to admit I was a bit insulted by the look of pain on his face.

"Good. I don't mean to hurt your feelings, but for my own safety I'm going to have to ask you to keep at least three feet away from me at all times."

"What are you talking about?"

Karl watched me thoughtfully as if debating what to tell me. "Do you remember the night that you were attacked by the golem?"

I grimaced. "It features regularly in my nightmares."

"The sheriff is the most controlled person I know. I've seen him in high pressure situations and not breaking a sweat, but the second that golem got its hands around your throat all bets were off. The fact we now know that you are his Destined Beloved makes sense of that night, and it's probably what triggered his berserker rage. Until everything is sorted out between the two of you, I'm going to be keeping my distance. I'd also suggest you keep away from any life-threatening situations. I think we'll all live much longer and happier lives if you do."

7

*B*y the time Tilda dragged me out of the library for lunch, I was ready to scream. It seemed that every member of the coven had wanted to see the woman who was the subject of a Destined Beloved vision by the Seer. If I hadn't known how rare an event it was before, I did now. It also seemed that being the subject of such a vision also made my love life a matter of public interest. There had been suggestions, lots of suggestions, some of them disturbing when you considered the source was a woman old enough to be my grandmother. Even escaping to the diner for lunch didn't provide me with any respite. Once again, everybody in the diner had their opinion on the subject.

"We need to get out of here," I muttered after I'd inhaled lunch in the shortest amount of time possible.

To her credit, Tilda didn't argue, she just grabbed her cone of silence stone and followed me out. I was so intent on getting out of the diner that I literally ran into the most attractive man I had ever seen in my life. I stepped back because I was pretty sure running my hands up his muscular arms would be considered socially unacceptable.

"I'm really sorry," I said as I tried to discreetly ensure I wasn't drooling.

"Don't be," he said in a deep voice that sent shivers through me. "I'm beginning to think that today was my lucky day." He smiled and showed a set of perfectly straight white teeth to go with the unearthly good looks. "I'm Todd, and I am very pleased to have you fall into my arms."

If I had to make a wild guess, I was betting he was a werewolf. According to everybody I knew in this town, nobody seemed to exude as much confidence when it came to flirting as the werewolves.

I grasped his outstretched hand. "I'm Sadie Goodwin."

Instantly my hand was dropped, and he stepped around me in a seemingly desperate attempt to put as much distance between us as possible. "Nice to meet you," he mumbled. "Bye."

I couldn't help but gape at his impression of an Olympic sprinter. "What's his problem?" I asked Tilda who seemed to be trying to unsuccessfully hold back laughter.

"You're the Sheriff's Destined Beloved now. The Seer couldn't have destroyed your love life more effectively if she'd slapped a chastity belt on you with a combination lock and biometric scanning upgrade."

"This isn't funny," I muttered between gritted teeth.

Tilda's facial contortions to try to hold in the laughter that was bubbling up inside her was truly an interesting sight. "Of course, it's not funny. It's terrible."

"You're not being very convincing," I said, dryly. "Seriously, just let it out. You're going to hurt yourself if you don't."

Tilda laughed heartily, bending at the waist as she tried to gulp in some air. "Did you see how fast he moved?"

"Yes, I did. It was truly impressive."

Tilda straightened up, wiping the tears from her eyes. "If

it makes you feel any better, you dodged a bullet on that one. Todd is every stereotype of a faithless werewolf come to life."

"But he was so pretty," I said as I looked down the street, wondering how far he'd get before he stopped running. "Where is this Seer?"

"Why?"

"I just want to have a chat to her about the prophecy."

"Seer's don't do take-backs on prophecies," Tilda said seriously. "If that's what you want, you are going to be sorely disappointed."

"I realize that, but everything has got a loophole. I just want to see where the loopholes for a Destined Beloved are."

Tilda groaned. "I don't think you're quite getting what a prophecy is all about."

IT WAS with great trepidation that I found myself standing at the front door of one of the strongest witches in Walker Bay. After ringing the doorbell, it occurred to me that this may not be one of my better ideas. It was a great idea just after lunch, but now it was the early evening and I'd had a whole afternoon working at the library to reconsider my options. Just when I was thinking I should turn around and walk away, the door opened and I had to admit that the woman who opened it was not what I was expecting.

"Uh, I'm looking for the Seer."

The woman who answered the door sighed heavily. "That would be me, but I prefer to go by Agnes, because it is my name, although nobody bothers to use it. What can I do for you, Sadie?"

I was surprised that she knew who I was, but I probably shouldn't have been. She was the Seer after all, although this was not the Seer I was expecting. I thought I'd find an older

37

lady, weighed down by all she had seen and the responsibility of her position. What I got was a woman about my age who had embraced the goth lifestyle. Her hair was black, short and spiky, as were most of her clothes. Tattoos wound their way down her arms and up her neck.

"I just wanted to have a chat with you about a prophecy you did that involved me."

"That would be the Destined Beloved prophecy. Sorry if you're not happy with it. All prophecies are final. No refunds or take backs, or whatever it is you're looking for."

"You realize that you've royally screwed up my life."

Agnes smiled. Not in an enigmatic way that I would have expected from a Seer. No, this was the mischievous smile of a child who knows they've created a huge mess, but can't find it in themselves to express regret because they had so much fun doing it.

"Look, I can do a reading on you to see if there are any details I missed on the first vision, but that's the best I can give you."

I nodded eagerly at the offer. I was really having difficulty adjusting to having my life determined by fate, maybe a reading would help.

I followed Agnes into the house and obediently sat down on the couch opposite her. She sat next to me, held my hands and looked into my eyes for a maximum of three seconds.

"Yup, prophecy still holds."

I yanked my hands back. "That's it? I thought you were going to do another reading."

The Seer heaved a sigh. "Despite what you want to think, I don't get prophecies wrong, I'm good at my job. If I tell you something, that is what's going to happen."

"Then why did you say you'd do a reading?"

Agnes snorted. "Because you're one of those people who think they're in control of their lives." She rolled her eyes.

"Control freaks are the worst people to deal with when it comes to prophecies. You always think you can find a loophole."

I stood up and started pacing. "This whole thing is ridiculous. I barely know the man. I'm sure I'm not his type, and what kind of a name is Destined Beloved anyway?"

Agnes shrugged. "Centuries ago some witch came up with the name that he or she thought sounded romantic. Just because we're witches doesn't mean we can't be geeky too."

I slumped back on the couch. "There's nothing that will change the prophecy?"

Agnes patted my hand gently and, for the first time, I saw some sympathy in her expression. "I can't begin to understand what you're going through, and if there was a way to modify it, I would tell you, but there isn't."

"You're sure this isn't something Flora pushed you into doing?" I couldn't help the suspicion that had been forming ever since my aunt had made the announcement at the Council meeting.

"I'm pretty certain that somebody has told you that Seer trumps coven leader every time. I tell her what to do, not the other way around."

"Great."

Agnes smiled. "If it makes it any better, it was a really nice vision. Usually my visions are full of death and destruction. Your vision was hot, and a little sweet, but mostly hot."

I wasn't quite sure what to say about that revelation.

"Gotta say, it shocked the hell out of me to have a vision about a Destined Beloved for the sheriff," she continued.

"Why, don't Seers get them all the time?"

"Not really. Believe it or not, soul mates are kind of rare, especially among werewolves. I can't even remember the last time a Seer had a Destined Beloved vision for a werewolf. They're not exactly into the whole soul mate thing. They really seem to like to spread the love, if you know what I mean."

"So I've heard."

"The sheriff is probably as upset over this as you are."

Strangely, that didn't help me. "You're saying that there is nothing I can do about it?"

Agnes shook her head. "That's not what I'm saying. You still have free will. You can fight against it. You can move away, find someone else and live your life on your terms."

I let out a breath I hadn't even known I'd been holding. "Thank goodness. So, everything will be okay. I just need to ignore the prophecy."

Agnes tilted her head. "I didn't say everything would be okay. No matter how you live your life, no matter how much you care about another person, you will always know that there is a piece missing from your soul, and you will always ache for that piece. Tossing away your Destined Beloved is not something to do lightly. I've only heard of one case where it was done successfully, and in that case one of the couple was a serial killing psychopath." She gave me a tight smile. "If my soul mate was like that, I'd be willing to give up a piece of my soul just to keep away from him."

"Assuming the sheriff isn't a serial killing psychopath, you're telling me that I have a choice, but it's a lousy one."

"Basically."

"Well, that's just great."

"You want romance and flowers, I am definitely not the person to ask. I deal in facts, and the fact is the sheriff is a good guy who fills out his uniform very nicely. I'm having trouble understanding why you're not jumping on that train."

I grimaced. "I don't take well to being told what to do."

"And the sheriff is one of the most dominant men around." Agnes snickered. "This is going to be fun. Not for you. It's going to be painful for you, but it's going to be hilarious for the rest of us."

I slapped my hands on my knees and stood up, frustrated that this visit hadn't gone the way I had been hoping. "Well, thanks for your time, I guess."

"You're leaving already?"

I frowned at the disappointment I heard in Agnes's voice. "Yeah, Tilda's taking me to some bar tonight for dinner. I have a feeling she knew how this meeting was going to play out."

"Oh, that sounds nice."

There it was again. That note of disappointment. As I looked around, I noticed the simplicity of the cottage. There were no photos of family or friends. Nothing to indicate she had a life outside her role as Seer. Until now, I had only been hearing about the reverent position held by the young woman sitting in front of me. I hadn't really thought about how isolating that power might be. She hadn't invited me into her house because she could change the prophecy. She invited me in because she was lonely. My heart clenched. I knew that feeling. When my mother died several months ago, I'd learned what true loneliness felt like. When I noticed the frozen dinner that was sitting on her kitchen bench, I knew I had to do something. "Would you like to come with us?" I blurted out.

Agnes looked shocked. "You want me to go out with you?"

"Sure," I said. "It's not a date or anything, I just thought you'd like to grab something to eat."

"But nobody ever wants to be around me. They're afraid of what I'll see."

I shrugged. "You already killed my romantic future by matching me with an uptight berserker with control issues. What else could you possibly do to me?"

"I could have a vision about your death."

A shiver went up my spine at the seriousness of her tone. "If you do, I'd suggest you keep that little nugget of information to yourself."

She appeared to consider that for a moment. "I'd love to go out to dinner with you," she said with all the solemnity of someone who had been asked to a royal wedding.

I hoped the evening lived up to her expectations.

8

*Y*ou know that moment on an old western movie when a stranger walks into a saloon and everyone goes silent. That's what happened when Tilda, Agnes and I walked into the local bar in Walker Bay.

"Why is everyone looking at us?" I muttered to Tilda.

"How should I know?" she replied as she led us to a table. "I mean, why would they stare at the Destined Beloved of their berserker sheriff, and the Seer who never, and I mean never, ventures from her home? This is just another normal day in Walker Bay."

"You know, sarcasm is not an attractive trait."

Tilda grunted in reply, her eyes sweeping the bar.

When we sat down I noticed that the noise level started to rise again, but there were still furtive looks thrown in our direction.

"How long do you think this is going to last for?" I couldn't overstate how uncomfortable the attention was making me.

Tilda snorted as she glared at people who were openly staring at us. "People fear anything that happens outside of their normal. A Destined Beloved vision and the Seer going bar hopping is pretty much outside everyone's version of normal. I'm just kind of grateful that I have a front row seat."

"I understand me, I've been getting weirdness all day." I looked over at Agnes. "Why are you getting so much attention?"

Agnes started twisting a napkin into knots. "I come from a family of Seers. We're kept separate from everyone else from birth, I don't go out socially, I was even home schooled. Up until today, my only social interactions consisted of the coven leader coming to see me for a prophecy."

"That sounds like a prison sentence." I couldn't help the frown that crossed my face.

"It is important that the Seer remains separate from coven life." Agnes sounded as if she was reciting a lesson from a holy book.

"So, you coming out with us tonight…?"

"Is considered a serious break in Seer tradition. This little excursion is going to have consequences. Serious consequences," I could tell Tilda was not happy.

I lowered my voice. "You mean we're now considered the bad influence?"

Tilda nodded, her expression grave.

"That is so cool. I've never been the bad influence before. Can I get a tattoo, you know, to warn all the other innocent Seers?"

Agnes started giggling and it was good to see a break in the serious expression I had seen her wearing.

Tilda sighed. "The worst part is that I just know I'm going to get blamed for this. I can just hear them now. 'Sadie's new in town, she doesn't know that dragging the Seer to a bar is the wrong thing to do. You know better, Tilda.' It's like I can hear Grandma's voice in my head."

"I can go home, I don't want to be any trouble." The look

on Agnes's face was heartbreaking, like a child who just had their ice cream snatched from their hands.

"She doesn't mean it." I glared at Tilda who looked slightly chagrined.

"I didn't," Tilda said apologetically. "I just don't deal well with change. Give me a few minutes. I'll be good after the first drink."

Sure enough, it only took one drink for Tilda to start to relax. Agnes took her time with hers, and I went for a soda so I could drive us home. I may have been the bad influence, but I was a responsible bad influence. It also gave me the opportunity to watch various members of the Walker Bay community without the interference of an alcoholic haze. I was learning a lot.

"Is it just me or are we getting dirty looks from just about every woman in this bar?" I asked.

"Oh, those looks aren't directed at us," Tilda said as she sipped her drink. "They're directed at you."

"What did I do?"

"Rumor has it that our sheriff was quite the werewolf in high school. It was like he had something to prove and he went about proving it in the most determined way possible. You might want to ask him about it before you take the next step in your relationship. You know the whole werewolves and spots thing." She waved her hand in the air and barely missed the tray carried by one of the passing waitresses.

"Even I knew about his exploits," piped up Agnes who had been paying serious attention to her drink, "and, as you've discovered, I had less access to town gossip than a nun in a cloistered convent."

"Is he still like that?"

Tilda shook her head. "He's been a little more discriminating since he came back to town, although that hasn't discouraged the attentions of those who want him to relive his high school glory days."

"That's not good," I said, a ball of worry developing in the pit of my stomach. "The last thing I want is to be anywhere near a player. I barely survived the last time. I refuse to go through that again."

Tilda's eyes narrowed. "There's a story there that you haven't told us. This might be the time to start."

I shook my head. "It's a part of my past and I don't ever want to revisit it. Suffice to say, I will run in the opposite direction if the sheriff is like that. Prophecy or no prophecy."

"Oh no, here comes trouble," Tilda said quietly, a worried look on her face.

"What?" I twisted my head and saw two women headed in our direction with determined expressions on their face. "Who are they?"

"They're from the other coven," Agnes looked just as concerned as Tilda.

"That still doesn't answer my question."

"You saw Myra in all her glory last night. Thanks to her mom being one of the coven leaders, she has a strong belief in her own importance, and she is just as unpleasant one-on-one as she is in a group setting. With her is her best friend, Jeanette, also the daughter of one of the coven leaders." Tilda said. "Both of them dated the sheriff in high school."

"From Myra's attitude towards the sheriff at the council meeting, I'm guessing it didn't end well," I muttered.

"It was a mess," Tilda said quietly. "She could not believe that he dumped her, and she took it badly. The drama kept us entertained for weeks."

"How about the other one?"

"Jeanette indulged in a spot of stalking when he left her in the dust. Ilsa and Violet had to get involved before it got really ugly."

I glared at Agnes. "What have you got me into?"

For the first time, Agnes's eyes flashed with anger. "Why does everyone blame the Seer. I'm just the messenger. If you've got a problem with the message, take it up with the Fates."

"Sorry," I grimaced. "Didn't mean to take it out on you."

"Heads up," muttered Tilda before swinging around with the most fake smile I had ever seen. "Myra, Jeanette, what a surprise to see you here."

"Good evening, Tilda," Myra replied but her eyes were glued to Agnes and me. "Care to introduce us to your friends."

"Of course, this is Sadie, she's new to the coven, and also Flora's niece. I would have thought you'd know Agnes, seeing as she's the Seer who has lived in this town her entire life."

I thought Tilda's smile was fake, but this woman's beat it, hands down. "Naturally, I know Agnes, I was just surprised to see her out here, and I was concerned. This atmosphere cannot be good for her. It's disappointing to see the lack of regard you have for the Seer."

"The Seer is perfectly capable of taking care of herself." Agnes surprised all of us by interrupting the staring contest that Myra and Tilda were having.

"And of course, we know of the sheriff's new conquest," Jeanette said. If looks could kill I'd be down on the ground.

"Well, actually…," I started.

"You do realize you're one of many," she continued as if I hadn't spoken. "One thing about Conall, he never stays with one girl for long. That's the thing with werewolves, they're usually not known for hanging in there long-term, but I'm sure you're going to find out all about that."

Even though I tried not to show any reaction to her statement, I could tell by the smirk on her face that I had not been successful.

"Really, Jeanette, are you that desperate for any attention from the sheriff that you want to take on his Destined Beloved?"

I had to say I was impressed. Tilda was in full protective mode tonight.

"We all know how she got the position," Myra said snidely and I felt like I'd been slapped.

"For the love of the Fates. What's your problem, Myra?" Tilda was just tipping over into seething mode.

"My problem is that the Seer so conveniently had a Destined Beloved vision for Flora's niece and the sheriff, just like her grandmother had a prophecy that deprived the rightful coven leader of her place."

Tilda stood to her full height and fixed a furious gaze on Myra and her friends. "Are you questioning the Seer?"

I glanced over at Agnes and the two of us started standing as well. I wasn't altogether familiar with bar fights, but I was pretty sure that this was how they started.

"Is there a problem here, ladies?" A deep voice interrupted our standoff.

"Of course, there isn't, Sheriff. We were just discussing coven business," Myra said, refusing to look away from Tilda.

"You, better than anyone, know that coven business should not be conducted in a bar," Sheriff Tolan drawled. "Things have a tendency to get heated, and that never plays well when alcohol is involved."

I glanced over at Jeanette to find her flicking her hair and smiling coyly at Sheriff Tolan. "It's so good to see you, Conall. Would you like to join us for a drink?"

"No."

There was silence as we all stood there waiting for someone to speak.

"Enjoy your evening, I'm sure we can continue this

discussion at another time." Myra said abruptly as she dragged a protesting Jeanette away from the group.

"What has happened to my town when Tilda Atwill is dragging the coven's newest member and the Seer into a bar brawl?"

"I wasn't exactly dragging them, they stepped up," Tilda said, pride evident in every word.

Sheriff Tolan frowned. "That wasn't the response I was hoping for."

Tilda did not look at all remorseful at his words, and the sheriff sighed, his irritation obvious.

"Miss Goodwin, may I have a word?"

"Of course, Sheriff Tolan."

"Not here, come with me."

I threw a panicked look at Tilda only to have her give me a thumbs up in return. I had a feeling I was not ready for this.

9

I followed the sheriff to an office at the back of the bar. I couldn't help the nervousness I felt as he closed the door behind us.

"Didn't think we needed an audience for this."

"What's going on, Sheriff?" I asked, cringing as I heard my voice crack.

Sheriff Tolan sighed and took his hat off, running a hand through his thick dark hair. "To start with, can you call me Conall? This whole situation seems just that bit weirder if you keep insisting on calling me Sheriff Tolan."

"Sure," I said. "You can call me Sadie if you want. I'm more likely to answer to that than Miss Goodwin anyway."

Conall paced across the room, his agitation obvious in every step. "I don't know what to do with this prophecy."

"I'm with you on that one. I tried to get the Seer to take it back, but I wasn't very successful."

"Is that why you're trying to get her drunk?"

"I'm not trying to get her drunk. Anyway, she was pretty adamant that there weren't any take backs with her visions."

"I didn't think she would," he muttered.

"So, what do we do?" I was curious. I knew how I felt about the prophecy and I was assuming the sheriff felt the same way.

"We could get married," he said, watching me with an intensity I found unnerving.

I almost choked. That was not where I was expecting him to go. "Okay, for a start, any talk of marriage is a long way off, like over the horizon long way off. In fact, I would appreciate it if all talk of marriage ceased, because just you mentioning it is causing me to have chest pains."

"Alright," he said, "if we take marriage off the table, where do we go from here?"

"What do you want?" I asked suddenly. It was beginning to occur to me that the sheriff might actually hate the idea of being linked to me in this way. I knew I had been fighting the prophecy based on the principle that I did not like being forced into something I had not asked for, but I knew if I was honest with myself, there was a small part that was urging me to accept the fate the Seer had laid out for me.

He glared at me. "There's a part of me that wants to claim you as mine, right here, right now."

That was a little more honest than I was expecting.

"You've got control of that part, don't you?" I asked nervously as I stepped behind the desk, feeling slightly safer with the large piece of furniture between us.

"Barely," he said through gritted teeth. "I don't know if it's the prophecy, or whether it is the berserker thing, but I've had an intense attraction to you since the day we met, and it's only getting worse."

"But you hate the feeling that we're both being forced into this," I guessed.

He nodded. "You the same?"

I nodded with what was probably a little too much enthusiasm.

"Is it the berserker thing?" he asked. "I can understand why that would be making you a little hesitant. According to Karl, what happened the night you got attacked by the golem wasn't a pretty sight. You must have been horrified."

"Horrified isn't quite the word I'd use. I was grateful that you saved me."

"I don't want your gratitude," he said harshly.

"Too bad, I am grateful. You saved my life and I'm pretty sure it was at some cost to you." If he was being honest with me, the least I could do was be honest with him. "I do feel something for you. On the night when the golem attacked, when you turned back into you, you kissed me. I've never had a kiss like that. I know you don't remember it…"

"Believe me, I remember it," Conall growled.

Oh, okay then. "We could just ignore the prophecy," I suggested.

"Ignore it?" The confusion on Conall's face looked very out of place.

"Who says we have to do anything about it. Neither of us was prepared for the prophecy. There's nothing saying we have to fulfill it in a certain amount of time. Admittedly, there is some attraction between us, but that isn't enough for a lifelong commitment. I suggest that we just take each day as it comes, get to know each other before we take an irreversible step."

Conall thought about that for a minute as if contemplating the wisdom of just doing nothing. I could tell that it went against his nature to just sit back and not take charge of the situation.

"I think that might be a good idea." He drew in a deep breath. "Why don't we start again." He put a hand out in front of him. "My name is Conall. I know this situation is strange, but I would really like a chance to get to know you."

I hesitated for a moment before grasping the outstretched hand. "My name is Sadie and I'm pleased to meet you."

"I should probably let you get back to your friends before they send in a search party," he said, seemingly reluctant to relinquish my hand. I had to admit I wasn't too keen for him to let go either. I had a feeling our chances of ignoring the Destined Beloved prophecy for any length of time was due for failure if the heat rushing through me was any indication. I reluctantly pulled my hand back. I had to be smart about this and use my head rather than instinct, or I could get myself in trouble.

As we headed to the door, I stopped and asked a question that had been bothering me since Tilda filled me in on his past. "Are you sure? I've been hearing things about you and I'm guessing what Flora said about werewolves is true. I will walk away and risk losing part of my soul rather than chance getting involved with a guy who prefers to keep his options open."

Conall froze and rubbed the back of his neck.

"I think I can guess what you've been hearing, and I can't deny I didn't have the best reputation in high school. In my favor, I never dated either of the women you're out with tonight," he said defensively.

"And I'm guessing that had more to do with the fact that Agnes was home schooled and you're more than a little scared of Tilda's grandmother."

Conall nodded, a little shamefaced, but then he straightened. "I have never cheated on anyone. My past is not necessarily pretty, but I want you to know that I will do my best not to screw this up."

It wasn't exactly moonlight and roses, but as far as romantic declarations went, I'd heard of worse. "Okay," I said quietly, avoiding his eyes as I stepped past him towards the door.

"Sadie, wait," I heard him growl as I reached for the doorknob.

"Look, I understand, but I need you to know that if you play me, I will walk away. Nothing is worth going through that."

Conall turned me around gently and tipped my chin up so I could see his eyes. "I promise that I will do everything that is in my power to make sure you are never hurt."

He dipped his head slowly, giving me a chance to push away. When his lips touched mine, my eyes fluttered closed. Emotion rushed through me and I gripped his arms, trying to bring him in closer. As his lips moved over mine, I felt like I was falling into something that I had no understanding of, and I lost all sense of time. He pulled back and touched his forehead to mine, looking deeply into my eyes.

"That's not going slow," I said.

"For me, this is glacial," he murmured.

"And you had to ruin it by reminding me that you're the complete opposite to what I want."

"We'll see," Conall said, his eyes glittering.

I turned around and opened the door. "Something tells me I'm going to regret coming back to Walker Bay," I threw over my shoulder.

≈

"Well, well, well, if it ain't the coven's newest lapdog and his witch owner."

I drew up short at the throughly unpleasant man who was sitting at the bar. It took me a moment to realize that Eamon was sitting next to him.

"Shut it, Brian. I don't have time for you." Conall's voice had taken on a hard edge that I had never heard before.

This had to be the infamous Brian Tolan that was

supposed to be our new sheriff before Flora destroyed the werewolf clan's plan. If I looked really hard I could see the family resemblance. They had the same chocolate brown hair and they both held themselves in the same way, but that was where the resemblance ended. Where Conall had a strength about him that inspired confidence, Brian made me feel uneasy. His brown eyes, so different from Conall's pale blue ones, studied me and a leery smile crossed his face as he glanced at the office we just came out of.

"I guess there had to be some perks. Hope the job is worth the leash you put around your neck," he sneered.

"Oh man," muttered Eamon. "Why did you have to go and do something stupid? I was just beginning to relax."

"Just go home, Brian, and sleep off whatever bitterness you're feeling right now," Conall said harshly. "Even if the coven hadn't taken me in, the town would never accept you as sheriff."

I tried to slip past the two men. I knew that whatever was going on between them started long before I turned up in town.

Brian caught my arm. "You know he'd do anything for that job, even seduce a woman he wouldn't normally look at twice."

Before I had a chance to process what he was saying, he was pulled away from me and Conall slammed him face down on the bar, his arm twisted up behind his back. I think we were all shocked by the feral look on Conall's face.

"You never touch her," he hissed.

Eamon put his hand on Conall's back. "Man, don't do this now. You're scaring her."

Conall glanced up at me, and something in my face must have got through because he pulled back from wherever he was going and yanked his brother up. "Your night is finished." He nodded to me as he dragged one brother out of the bar with another brother trailing behind him.

I walked over to Tilda and Agnes, aware that every set of eyes in the bar was watching me. I sat down quietly and sipped my drink as if nothing had happened.

"Okay," drawled Tilda, "that was hot, a little concerning maybe, but really hot."

I dropped my head on the table. "I can't believe I'm stuck in the middle of this."

Tilda rubbed my back in what I was assuming was supposed to be a sympathetic gesture. "You've definitely made life more interesting around here. You want to tell us what you were doing in the back room of the bar with the sheriff."

"You know, when you say it like that, it sounds like we were doing something wrong."

Tilda chuckled. "I saw your face when you first came out of the office, I'm pretty sure there was something going on."

"We were just talking," I lied. There was no way I wanted to go into details about that kiss, not until I was sure that it was honest emotion, and not the fact that I had been played by a master.

"So, what did you talk about, or do?" Tilda looked over at Agnes and winked. "We want details, lots of details."

"We discussed the prophecy and we've decided that for now we're going to ignore it."

"You're ignoring my prophecy?"

I looked around and tried to quieten Agnes as her voice rose.

"Do you have any idea what a prophecy does to me? I get headaches and every muscle aches, and you're just going to ignore it."

"Please don't take it personally," I pleaded. "It's just that neither of us are ready to deal with it, so we're just going to put it aside for now."

"Considering the whisker burn on your face, I'm not sure whether you're really grasping the whole concept of putting it aside," Tilda stated.

I grunted, choosing to ignore what she said.

"I have a plan for you," Tilda stated.

"You can get me out of this?"

"No, but we are going to blow off some steam tonight. Let's forget everything and worry about it tomorrow."

"Because that always works," I said morosely.

"Trust me."

Agnes and I exchanged looks. There was no way this was going to end well.

$\mathcal{M}$y night had ended with me wrangling a seriously inebriated and belligerent Seer into her bed and hoping that she'd stay there. Between that and dealing with Tilda who was sure the world was going to end because we'd corrupted the Seer, I'd finished the night with a headache that I was sure would rival the hangover pain my companions were going to wake up with. Maybe that was why I assumed the pounding I heard when I dragged my eyes open was completely in my head. It didn't take long for me to work out that someone badly wanted to get into my house. Knowing my luck, Tilda was right, and the coven was at my door with pitchforks, ready to punish me for taking their most venerated member bar hopping. I headed carefully down the creaking stairs only to jump when I heard a crash. I raced the rest of the way to the ground floor. When thinking about it later I knew that it was the absolute worst thing that I could do, but in my defense I was still half asleep and not thinking clearly. Downstairs, I found Conall and Karl about to head up to my bedroom, their eyes wild.

"What the hell is going on?"

Karl put his hands on his knees and bent over, his eyes closed. "Thank the Fates."

Conall didn't say a word, he just stood there and watched me as if afraid I was going to disappear.

"Are you going to tell me what is going on?" I asked.

"We found a body in the park overlooking the bay, near the bench where you usually sit in the mornings," Karl replied.

"Who was it?"

"That's the thing, we couldn't identify who it was, all we could see was that it was a female."

I glanced over to where Conall was leaning against the wall, gulping in air as if he'd run a marathon. "You thought it was me, didn't you?"

Karl nodded.

I walked over to where the sheriff was obviously trying to calm down.

"This doesn't mean I've changed my mind about anything, but I think you need it," I said as I leaned my head against his chest and wrapped my arms around him. I heard the way his heart was racing, and when he returned the embrace I could feel his body shaking.

"I thought I'd lost you," he whispered, his voice bleak.

"I know," I replied as I rubbed his back, trying to provide as much comfort as I could. "I'm safe. I had a late night and slept in. I was nowhere near the park."

"But you could have been."

He was right. If it hadn't been for the late girl's night with Tilda and Agnes I would have been sitting on that bench. Chances are I would have been a witness or a victim, neither of which were good options.

I pulled back slightly, as far as Conall would allow.

"What did you do to my door?"

He glanced back at the piece of wood that was now

hanging precariously from one hinge. "When you didn't answer I kind of lost my head," he said.

Great, I'd lived in this house less than forty-eight hours and I was pretty sure my landlord was not going to be happy. I'd have to make sure it was fixed before Flora found out about it.

"What did you do to my door?"

I really couldn't take a trick. I peered around the sheriff to find my great aunt examining what was left of her front door. "Good morning, Flora. How can I help you this morning?"

"You can tell my why my door looks like you had a wild party here last night after dragging the Seer through the depths of depravity.

"It was one bar and I swear she only had about two and a half drinks. The woman is a lightweight and that is clearly not my fault."

Conall raised one of his hands to interrupt me, keeping the other arm firmly wrapped around my waist. "The door is my responsibility. I'll get it fixed."

Flora eyed the two of us, seemingly wrapped in each other's arms. "I'm missing something here, aren't I?"

"I'll explain later." I pulled away from Conall and could feel the reluctance radiating from him. I lowered my voice. "You need to go back to your job. You've checked on me and I'm safe. I know the prophecy is messing with you, but you have a murderer to find."

He nodded sharply. "Give me your phone," he ordered.

At this stage, arguing just for the sake of arguing seemed to be a bit of a petty move to make, so I grabbed my purse that I had left downstairs the night before and passed him my phone.

"I'm putting my number in as an emergency contact. If you need me for anything, I want you to contact me immediately. I don't care if it's because you stubbed your toe, I want to hear about it from you, nobody else. Do you understand?"

"Yes," I said meekly. I could see that this morning's events had left him on edge. Sometimes it's just easier to agree in the moment and sort out the details at a later time when everybody is back on a normal emotional keel.

He handed back my phone and gave me a quick hug before turning and stalking out of the house.

"Please don't call us if you stub your toe," Karl muttered. "Today is going to be a horror show of a day, the last thing he needs is distractions."

I rolled my eyes. "Please, like I'm that much of an idiot. You saw what he was like, if he wanted me to agree that the sky was green, I would have. Just keep an eye on him."

For the first time that morning Karl smiled, showing pointy teeth that no longer disturbed me. "I think you're going to be good for him." He started to follow his boss out before stopping and turning. "Also, unless you want to see him lose it completely, next time you hear a noise like somebody is breaking into your house, do not investigate what it was. Get out of the house and call us. Trust me, when he starts thinking properly, he is going to go nuts that you came downstairs to confront us."

"Understood," I saluted.

"I can see you're going to be a lot of work," he muttered as he skirted around Flora.

"Did you want to explain what happened here at this unearthly hour?" Flora asked as soon as Karl left.

"A body was found up at the park that overlooks the bay. There was some concern that it was me."

Flora frowned. "How could they not know?"

I shrugged, not liking the visual that came to mind after what Karl had told me. "They weren't able to identify the body, and since I have been making a habit of walking up there early in the morning, an assumption was made that it could have been me. Apparently, the sheriff didn't react well, and nothing was going to stop him from finding out whether I was safe."

"That explains the door," grumbled Flora.

"I'll organize to get it fixed first thing this morning," I assured her.

"Unfortunately, you won't," she said. "You and I need to have a talk."

I dropped down on the couch and motioned to her to join me. "Talk away."

Flora shook her head. "Not here, this is important...too important to risk anyone overhearing."

I looked around at my slightly decrepit house. "Who is going to hear us?"

"You'd be surprised," she said sagely. "Now get dressed and make sure you're wearing something that's comfortable for hiking.

11

"When you said wear something for hiking, I didn't realize you meant we'd be doing this for hours," I grumbled as I struggled for breath.

"It's not too far now," encouraged Flora, who to my great embarrassment sounded less out of breath than I did. I had a feeling I was going to need to up my visits to the gym if fitness was a requirement for witches.

"I'm having a little trouble understanding what is going on here. If you don't want anyone to hear what we are saying, why don't you just get the cone of silence stone from Tilda. We use that in the diner all the time and nobody can hear us."

Flora snorted. "For the conversation we are about to have I want to go somewhere where we have complete privacy." She pointed further up the hill. "If you could pick up the pace a bit, we should be able to get there in another ten minutes, more or less."

"Okay," I breathed out, despite the sneaking suspicion that she was trying to kill me.

She lied. It was another thirty minutes before we reached

the clearing and I was able to collapse on the ground, lying on my back in the grass as I tried to drag some sweet oxygen into my lungs.

"You should exercise more," Flora said as she bustled around the outskirts of the clearing, placing items at intervals and doing hand movements above them.

"What are you doing?" I decided to ignore the judgment I could feel emanating from her about my fitness level. As far as I was concerned, today's little expedition was going to cover my exercise quota for the next month.

"I am creating a magic circle so that we can talk privately."

I struggled into a sitting position. "Isn't this a bit dramatic for a simple conversation?"

Flora lowered herself to the ground in front of me. "No, this is a conversation we've been putting off, and this morning I found out that we have run out of time."

"What has happened?" I could hear my voice rising an octave, but I could see true fear in Flora's eyes. Whatever she had to tell me was not going to be good.

"The Conclave is sending a magister to examine what happened with Isobel and the curse she put on me."

The tone in Flora's voice had an ominous quality that filled me with dread. "What is a magister, and why is that news so bad that we had to hike through mountains to find somewhere you could tell me about it?"

"Magisters are the police of the witch world. They work for the Conclave and their job is to bring in rogues for trial in front of a tribunal." Flora looked away as if contemplating what to say next. "They also have the power to execute certain witches who are deemed too dangerous to bring to the Conclave."

My jaw dropped. "That sounds like the worst way for a civilized society to run its justice system."

Flora grimaced. "That's because the Conclave came into being at a time when civilized society did not exist, and they keep those rules regardless of the changes that have happened in the rest of the world."

My face must have looked as confused as I felt because Flora rubbed her hands over her face. "This isn't working, I need to remember that you are completely new to our world and all the information you've been getting has been random snippets. That stops now. If you're going to survive, you need to know more about the world you are in right now." She stood up and started pacing. "Witchcraft has been around since the beginning of time. Nobody knows when it started or how it started, but our archaeologists are still finding evidence of primitive spell castings in caves, so as far as we know the paranormal world has been developing right alongside normal people for the entire extent of human history. Like human history ours has parts that we aren't particularly proud of. Unfortunately, when you have people with power, there will always be a certain number who will abuse it."

"How badly?" I asked.

Flora looked down at the ground and swallowed. "Have you heard about the Black Death plague that spread through Europe in the fourteenth century?"

I had a bad feeling where this was going. "Millions of people died."

Flora nodded sadly. "Normal humans have always been more populous than paranormals. We will always be outnumbered. There was a group - a small group - who decided they needed a way to even the odds. At the center of that group was the greatest cursebreaker the world has ever known. She was the reason that cursebreakers became so reviled in the paranormal world."

"Wait a second, weren't witches blamed and hunted for

the Black Death anyway? Doesn't that seem a little self-defeating?"

"Normal women were accused of being witches," Flora corrected. "Throughout history, very few witches have actually been victims of the witch hunts. Most of those killed were women and some men who had simply angered the wrong person." Flora drew in a breath. "The Middle Ages was a terrible time for witchcraft. Dark magic users multiplied. Curses were cast with no thought to their consequences, for the slightest things. There is one story of a teenage witch putting a curse on the entire family of a human girl simply because a boy they both liked had complimented the human girl. Anarchy reigned and there were no controls in place. The plague was the final straw. A group of very powerful witches who had managed to put an end to the plague before it completely wiped out the human population in Europe, decided that witches needed a government. They started with a small but powerful group of covens which provided representatives to the Conclave. Rules were written up that were designed to end the chaos. It took centuries but witchcraft finally was brought under control."

"I know I'm going to regret asking this, but how was a small group of witches able to bring the whole population under the control of the Conclave?" I had a bad feeling that I knew the answer to this.

"You need to remember that the Middle Ages were a horrific time in history, and the Conclave used those methods to bring control. The precepts were instituted as absolute laws and the punishment for breaking them was swift and brutal. It was the only way to bring in order." She looked away. "Now I think we cling to it simply because it's familiar and we're afraid of what will happen if we loosen the reins."

"And the magisters?"

"The magisters are among the strongest of the witches. They are answerable only to the Conclave and the precepts, nothing else matters to them. They are able to break through the abilities of most witches, they are able to use magic to convince people to become spies for them, and most importantly, they can see through lies to the truth."

"And that's why we're sitting on top of a mountain."

"It's not a mountain," Flora said impatiently. "This hill has natural qualities which amplify magical powers. I'm hoping it will help with bringing forth your natural abilities. We need that because now that you know that the Conclave takes breaches of the precepts very seriously, there is one precept that concerns us."

"Cursebreakers," I murmured.

"One of the final precepts to be added was the execution order for all cursebreakers. That happened about three hundred years ago. For the hundred years before that, there were some cursebreakers working for the magisters, dismantling the worst of the huge number of curses that had accumulated over the centuries. Once that work had been completed, all the cursebreaker families were eliminated for the greater good, to ensure we never saw those dark times again."

The clinical way she said it was more horrifying than the words themselves. It was like she had learned it by rote as a child and repeated it so often it was a part of her.

"How could they do that?"

"It was not a decision taken lightly. The thinking was there was no use dismantling the weapons if those that could build them up easily were left alive with the ability to do it. You need to understand that the worst of the curses were created by cursebreakers, and it didn't matter if the current generation was innocent, the next generation could contain the witch that destroyed the world. The risk was considered too great."

"You do realize how sick this all sounds to someone who has never heard the history. It sounds like genocide."

"It was genocide and you're right. Looking back at it with the morality of today, it was a crime and many have judged it as such. That doesn't change the outcome. The purge was complete. There is nothing that can be done. The last cursebreaker was killed centuries ago and the talent was only found in certain families. With them wiped out, the precept dealing with cursebreakers became one of those shameful pieces of history that we can point at to show just how civilized we've become." Flora watched me carefully.

"And you're worried how the Conclave is going to react if they find out that a cursebreaker has spontaneously been born into the modern age," I could see why she was concerned. After everything she'd told me I wasn't willing to risk my continued existence on the fact we supposedly lived in a more enlightened time. I'd seen what the internet was like, witch hunts and hysterical mobs were still very much a part of the human condition. I straightened my shoulders. "I need you to tell me what to do. Would it be better for me to get out of town for a while?" I didn't like that option, but the more I learned about the Conclave, the less I wanted to pop up on their radar.

"It's too late for that. Too many people know you were a witness to everything that happened. They will want to talk to you, and they won't take no for an answer."

I shivered despite the morning sun. "What am I going to tell them?"

"Definitely not the truth," Flora said grimly.

"You don't think the magister will be understanding when I tell him I was mugged by two senior citizens and dragged here against my will in the trunk of their car," I queried, a small smile tugging at my lips.

Flora grimaced. "If you value your life, I would suggest never referring to Margot and Maude as senior citizens. We need another story, preferably one where you were fully aware of the paranormal world your entire life and you were thrilled to be invited to Walker Bay to join the coven."

"I thought you said that magisters are able to see through lies." Not to mention I had always been terrible when straying from the truth, a facet of my personality that my mother had been eternally grateful for.

"Usually they are, but legend has it that cursebreakers are immune to truth scans, no matter how powerful the witch conducting them. Whatever you say should be believed."

"Legends?" Considering those legends had to be at least several hundred years old, I didn't know whether I wanted to depend on their accuracy.

Flora shrugged helplessly. "It's the best that I have, it isn't like I can call a friend and ask for advice. Normally I would ask for Maude's opinion, but we can't risk letting anybody know what you are." She gripped my arm. "You can never tell anybody." The fear in her voice was palpable.

"Then we better come up with a really good story, and I may need training in how to tell a convincing lie because that is not a part of my skill set."

Flora smiled gently. "Then we need to get started. Fortunately, we have a bit of time. Investigations never move quickly, so it could be a couple of weeks before they get to the point of interviewing people. By the time the magister shows up, you are going to be the most uninteresting apprentice witch Walker Bay has ever seen."

At least we had a plan.

*A*s we headed back to my house, I couldn't believe that we had only been gone one day. After we had concocted a believable story to tell to the magister, Flora had taken it upon herself to start my training in the art of witch-craft, just enough to prove that I had some knowledge and wasn't a complete novice when it came to this new world I had found myself in. My head pounded from trying to remember so much information, and my body ached from the excessive amount of exercise that had been poured into the day.

"Please tell me that was not a normal training day," I groaned as I laid my head against the car window.

"You think I still have the energy to do that every day," Flora grumbled.

"You seem to have more energy than I do." I had to admit to being slightly embarrassed at how much more fit my great-aunt seemed to be than I was. I really needed to start working out, if only to avoid the humiliation I was sure would be coming my way if anyone found out about today.

"Are you okay with the house?"

I was snapped out of my musings by the random question. I glanced over at Flora and saw a flash of guilt cross her face. "I like it, why? It isn't haunted is it?"

Flora shook her head. "No, but I have a sneaking suspicion that it may have a curse on it."

I glanced around, concerned that one of those paranormal beings with enhanced hearing was within eavesdropping distance.

"Don't worry," Flora said, "my car is warded. Casual listeners can't hear what we're saying."

I gave a sigh of relief until I remembered what she'd said. "You put me in a house with a curse attached to it. What exactly did I do to you to deserve such special treatment?"

"You're the only person who could live in it without it harming you. With any luck, you'll be able to break it."

It disturbed me that she showed no remorse at all.

"You know, considering curses have been outlawed for the last several hundred years, there sure seem to be a lot around."

Flora shrugged. "Yes, well, the war on drugs hasn't exactly been a raging success either. Banning things never works as well as people hope they do."

"What kind of curse am I looking at?"

Flora shrugged, her eyes glued to the road. "About thirty years ago the house was left to a young woman and her husband by her parents. Unfortunately, her younger sister had been living in the house and had let it get run down. According to the will, she needed to be evicted. Once the courts agreed, she left the house, but I believe she left a curse that meant that no woman would find happiness in the house."

"It was a will dispute?" I knew that I sounded incredulous, but seriously. "You people have all this power and yet you still have issues like will disputes in families."

"We're people, and some people do not react well to not getting their own way," Flora stated. "Especially in this case. The younger sister was furious, even though she had treated her parents like an open wallet her entire life. Her older sister had made it on her own without a cent from their parents. In their will they wanted to redress the balance."

"That was brave of them." I couldn't help the sarcasm in my voice. "They weren't strong enough to stand up to their daughter in their lifetime, so they left the mess for the responsible daughter to clean up."

"Yes, well, family can be messy," Flora sighed.

Having spent my entire life believing that my family consisted of just me and my mother, only to find out my family consisted of witches who were feuding, I was taking a crash course in dysfunctional families.

"Wait a minute, you have me living in a house that has a curse specifically targeting women."

Flora waved her hand. "You'll be fine. Like I said, you should be immune, and if you can get rid of the curse, you can keep the house."

My jaw dropped. "You're giving me a house?"

A laugh burst out of Flora. "At the moment that house is an albatross around my neck. I purchased it so one of the most responsible members of my coven would get some recompense out of the disaster her parents left her. Nobody has been able to live in it, and the younger daughter is long gone, so we can't get her to fix the mess she made. Unless you can do something, that house is going to rot until it falls down. Even then, chances are we won't be able to build on the land, as the curse has been there so long it's probably infecting the whole property. It is worthless to me, and at least this way I won't have to pay taxes on it anymore."

"You make it sound like curses are living things."

Flora tapped her finger on the steering wheel, the only

hint that she was nervous about our conversation. "When you saw the curse tablet, what did it look like?" she asked.

I remembered back to the first time I'd come face-to-face with evil. "Blackness, tendrils like snakes writhing on top of it." I swallowed as the visual that I had done my best to forget over the last two weeks once again surged to the forefront of my brain.

"That's pure malevolence, and if fed, it can grow. It is the main difference between spells and curses. Spells, no matter how mischievous they may be, don't have that core of evil to them, and they can't spread uncontrollably like a curse can if not properly crafted. Spells will just fizzle out if not attended to, but a curse can take on a life of its own." Flora shook her head. "A part of me has always understood why the Conclave was so brutal in outlawing curses and destroying anyone with the skills to craft the worst of them."

"And now?"

Flora looked over at me and her expression softened. "You got dragged into our world against your will. Despite that, you saved my life as well as my sanity. If anyone comes for you, they will need to go through me first." Her lips quirked upward in a smile. "Besides, you're the only member of my family that doesn't hate me on sight. I'm not letting that go."

"But you will let me live in a house with a curse on it," I said wryly.

Flora laughed. "Well, there's family, and then there's business."

*a*s we drove up to my curse house, I spotted something that I was not expecting.

"Looks like someone is taking his Destined Beloved responsibilities seriously," Flora noted as we pulled into the driveway.

On my front porch was the sheriff in unfamiliar civilian clothing, and it looked like he was doing construction work. "And here I thought my day couldn't get any stranger." A worrying thought crossed my mind. "This curse you think could be on my house, it won't hurt Conall, will it?"

Flora shook her head. "As far as I'm aware it was only targeting females, and you being there should mute it a little until you find it."

That sounded like the worst treasure hunt ever.

"You're working in the library tomorrow." Flora made it sound like an order and not a question. "We need an audit of all the grimoires. That needs to be your first priority. If Isobel wasn't destroying books with curses in them, we need to know where they are and if she was sharing the knowledge with anyone else."

I nodded as I opened the car door. "I'll get on it." I hesitated and glanced up at the sheriff who was now watching me. "Is there any way for me to close the library temporarily?"

Flora didn't look too thrilled.

"What you're asking is time intensive, and yesterday I had people constantly coming in and asking about the Destined Beloved prophecy. There is no way that I am going to be able to do the work you want if I keep getting distracted."

"You're the librarian, it's your choice. As long as you leave a number you can be contacted at so if someone has an emergency you can get there."

I stifled a laugh. "I never thought I'd work in a library where an emergency is a likely occurrence."

Flora grinned. "The world is an interesting place." She glanced over at the sheriff who seemed to be waiting patiently. "I think your Destined Beloved is waiting for you."

"Will you stop calling him that," I muttered as I slammed the car door. I could still hear her laughter as I walked over to the front door of my house which was back on its hinges. "What are you doing?" I asked as I tried not to get distracted by this rugged and handy version of the sheriff.

"I'm fixing the door I broke," he said simply.

"I get that, but aren't you supposed to be investigating a murder?"

"You'd think so, but I've been relieved of my duties until the state police can determine whether I should be charged with committing that murder."

"What?"

Conall looked around. "I'd really rather not discuss this out here, any chance of you inviting me inside for a coffee so we can talk?"

"Sure." I hoped the care package Tilda had left for me included coffee. I swung my new front door open and frowned. "This feels heavier." Then I saw the new security hardware. "What the...?"

Conall gave a sheepish smile. "I'm not sure if it will work against a frantically worried berserker, but it should keep most other people out."

He followed me into the house and, after I made coffees, we sat down on the couch. For a moment I reveled in the domestic scene, but a moment was all I was going to get.

"You need to start explaining what you said."

Conall sighed and leaned back. "The victim was Jeanette Hocking."

"Who?" He was looking at me as if I should know who he was talking about.

"You met Jeanette last night." He cleared his throat and looked a little embarrassed. "I believe she talked to you about the prophecy."

"Your stalker," I burst out, remembering the woman from the bar.

Conall's face colored. "She wasn't exactly a stalker, just a little confused."

I remembered the malice in the woman's expression when she glared at me the night before. There was more than just confusion there.

"She looks nothing like me, how could you have thought she was me?"

"Her body was torn to pieces," Conall said, his hand reaching for mine as if he needed that physical contact to ensure his nightmare hadn't come true. "Truth be told, I just panicked. I saw a body in a place where you normally sit, at a time you are normally there." He frowned. "This prophecy is messing with me more than I'd like to admit."

"I think I understand all that, but can we get to the part where you are a suspect and not the investigating officer."

Conall sighed and I could tell how frustrated he was. "The history between Jeanette and me is very well known in town. When her coven discovered that she was the one who had been murdered, they instantly accused me. Normally those kinds of unfounded accusations would be ignored, but her mother is one of the coven leaders. She went to the head of the werewolf clan..."

"Who immediately saw a way to get rid of you." I was learning to really hate politics.

"Yes, on top of the fact that the victim was torn to pieces and I have recently been outed as a berserker."

"So, you're telling me that you are being accused of murdering a woman based entirely on the fact that you're a berserker. There is no actual evidence that you did anything."

"That about sums it up," Conall said as he leaned back against the couch and closed his eyes.

"Can I ask you a personal question?"

"Considering half the town thinks we had sex in the back office of the bar last night, I'm pretty sure there are no personal questions between us anymore."

That gave me a sick feeling inside. I hated being the target of gossip. "Is that true?" I asked in a small voice.

"I think Myra and Jeanette started the rumor," Conall said, apologetically. "I'm sorry, I wasn't thinking. I shouldn't have tried to talk to you privately in such a public place."

"We were only in there for a short amount of time." I couldn't understand why anybody would say things that were so untrue.

"I'm guessing those people who believe the rumor aren't that impressed with me."

I knew he was trying to make me smile, but I was having trouble getting there.

"Why is your father doing this? I thought fathers were

supposed to be there for their kids. I know mine isn't, but he doesn't know I exist. Your father is a proper dad, isn't he? Why is he determined to get you out of this job?"

Conall stretched his neck from side to side and I heard a crack. "Now you're asking the hard questions."

I stayed silent, waiting for him to continue.

"I'm the youngest of five boys. The eldest is Eamon, then Garrett, then Patrick, then Brian, and then me, the runt." He smiled humorlessly. "Clan life is volatile. Fidelity isn't really a big thing, and over the years I learned that the alpha took full advantage of his position. He had the wife at home looking after his sons who were, for the most part, growing big and strong, so he could play the field. Nobody was going to question him, least of all my mother. She was always made aware of the privileged position she held as the wife of the alpha." He sighed and I could tell the memories were taking a toll. "When I didn't turn as a teenager the rumors started that I wasn't the alpha's son. According to the clan, my mom must have had an affair. That was the only explanation for my being defective. In public, my father never gave any indication that he thought there was a possibility I wasn't his son. In private, was another matter altogether."

"So, what happened?" I asked, desperately wishing I knew this man well enough to know how to comfort him. The bleak expression on his face told me more than his words ever would.

"One night, my mother took off and never came back."

"How old were you?" I asked.

"Fourteen. Most werewolves have their full change by the age of thirteen. The fact that I hadn't changed by fourteen meant that there was something seriously wrong. I was taken to a multitude of healers, but nobody knew what the problem was." He smiled ruefully. "I guess nobody thought that my being a berserker was a possibility." He glanced over at me thoughtfully. "I find it interesting that I'm both a berserker and part of a Destined Beloved prophecy. I've been wondering if that's normal."

"What do you mean?"

Conall watched me carefully, as if deciding what to tell me. "One day I will tell you more, but for now all you need to know is that in my life I have been in a lot of dangerous and terrifying situations. Not one of them triggered the berserker rage until I saw you struggling for your life against that golem." He rubbed his hand through his hair and the look in his eyes was tortured. A part of me was beginning to understand what the prophecy was doing to him. "I hadn't felt that helpless since I was a kid, and something just exploded inside me. I lost control, and I don't think anything could have brought me back except you. The berserker thing terrifies me, but I truly believe that you will always be able to bring me back. That's why, despite what we said last night, I believe in the Destined Beloved prophecy, and I believe that you are my salvation."

My mouth felt dry. That was a lot of responsibility.

Conall sighed. "I've freaked you out, haven't I?"

I held up my hands with a space about two feet between them. "A little bit."

He chuckled, and for the first time I could see a lessening of the tension around his eyes. "Just know I would never hurt you and we will go at whatever pace you are comfortable with."

I took in a deep breath to try to contain the nervousness that I felt. "Would you like to stay for dinner? We could order a pizza...I'm not much of a cook...that's something that I need to learn." I knew I was rambling but all of a sudden it was hitting me. Regardless of what I thought about the prophecy, this man and I were linked in a way that I was just barely beginning to understand.

Conall raised my hand and kissed it, sending all kinds of delicious feelings running through me. "I would like that very much."

In that moment, I had a feeling that no matter what I said about fighting the prophecy, my fate was sealed.

*M*y late night with Conall had not ended the way I had secretly hoped it would. Despite my protestations that I wanted to take things slowly, there was a part of me that was beginning to accept the prophecy. That part of me was not necessarily satisfied with the gentle kiss I had received when he left. The result was a night where I tossed and turned and barely got any sleep. As the sun crept over the horizon, I gave up on even trying. Remembering the way Conall had implored that I be careful, I knew that my going for a walk was more than he would be able to cope with. The last thing I wanted to do was to add to his current problems.

I was still in my pajamas and eating breakfast when there was a pounding on my door. I was beginning to wonder if this was going to turn into my standard wake-up routine. At least this time my door wasn't being ripped off its hinges. I was surprised to find Tilda was the one doing a fine impression of our local law enforcement officials. "What's the emergency?"

Tilda's mouth opened and closed but no words came out. She grabbed my arm and started pulling me outside.

"What are you doing?" I complained as she dragged me through the door. "I'm not even dressed yet."

She turned me around and I felt my mouth go dry. The words 'Your Next' were written in ominous dark red letters across the front of my house.

"I would have thought that if you put this kind of effort into threatening somebody, you would check that you got the spelling right."

Tilda rounded on me with an incredulous expression on her face. "Somebody's threatening you and you're critiquing their spelling?"

I shrugged weakly. I didn't know what else to do. I had never been overtly threatened like this in my life, and I had no idea how to deal with it. As I studied the words which were written in large letters so nobody could miss them, a sudden thought struck me. "That's paint, isn't it?"

I felt Tilda shiver and her hand sought out mine. I was grateful for the warmth because I was starting to feel a chill go through me that I was pretty sure had nothing to do with the weather.

"You think it could be blood?" she whispered.

I really hoped not. I tried swallowing the feeling of rising bile in my throat and tugged on her hand. "I'm going to call Conall. It must have happened after he left last night.

Tilda stopped in her tracks and I got yanked back by her hand. "I thought you were ignoring the prophecy."

"We are." Even I could hear how ridiculous that sounded. "He just came over to fix my door, we grabbed a pizza and talked for a bit."

Tilda smirked at the rising blush I could feel stealing across my cheeks and I could tell she was grateful for the distraction. "Sure, you just talked. I could get whiplash from trying to follow the changes in direction of this relationship."

I couldn't argue with her. My head was telling me that allowing myself to submit to the Destined Beloved prophecy was crazy and I should fight it with everything I had. Normal people do not follow the whims of prophecy, but every time I looked into those pale blue eyes of his I found myself succumbing.

"We'll work it out at some point, just please try to limit the mocking while we do."

"You don't know me at all, do you?"

I gave the requisite smile. I knew she was trying to distract me from the fact that somebody was targeting me, but I also knew my heart wasn't in it. Once we got back in the house, I scrambled to find my phone. I could feel my hands shaking as I held it up and waited for it to connect.

"Sheriff Tolan speaking." It amazed me how just the sound of his voice could calm my shattered nerves.

"I need you to come to my house."

Before I launched into an explanation, he cut me off with a terse growl. "I'm on my way. Find somewhere safe and wait for me." With that he hung up.

I looked down at my now disconnected phone and then up at Tilda. "He hung up on me."

Tilda shook her head and started pushing me upstairs. "He's a man of action, not words. If you are going to stay with him, I would suggest you develop a group of friends who can assist with your emotional needs. I can guarantee that man is not going to be able to help you in that area. Now get dressed. From the sounds of it, the cavalry is coming."

I wasn't sure what she was talking about until I heard the approaching sound of sirens filling the early morning silence. A part of me cringed. I was not going to be popular with my new neighbors. By the time I threw on some clothes and raced downstairs, I found Karl standing next to Tilda on the road, glaring at the writing on my house as if it was a personal affront to his sensibilities.

"You okay?" he asked as he looked me up and down.

"I didn't even know it happened until Tilda turned up and showed me." I shivered at the thought that somebody with evil intent against me had been just outside my house while I was sleeping and vulnerable.

A truck came barreling down the street and the tires screeched as it came to a sudden halt.

"And this is the point where it is all going to go to hell," muttered Karl as we watched a furious sheriff stalk towards me.

"Report," he barked as he grabbed me and held on tight.

As Karl gave Conall the small amount of information we had, I could feel his hands stroking up and down my back. Despite the less than ideal circumstances, I had never felt as safe in my entire life as I did in his arms. I looked up at him and asked the one question which had been plaguing me since I first saw the writing.

"Is that paint?"

I could tell from the look in Conall's eyes that I wasn't going to like the answer to my question. He lowered his head until our foreheads were touching, his hands gently stroking the sides of my face. "It's blood, sweetheart."

My eyes closed as I took that in. I heard a door slam.

"This can't be good," I heard Tilda mutter.

"Sheriff Tolan," an authoritative voice called. "You know you are not permitted at crime scenes."

I stiffened at the slight.

Conall didn't even lift his head. He kissed me gently on the side of my face and whispered in my ear. "I'm really sorry for what is about to happen, just trust that we are a team, no matter what anybody says." He straightened his shoulders, reached for my hand, and turned to face the new arrival.

I couldn't believe my luck. I had just rolled out of bed and barely thrown on the closest clothes I could find, and I was faced with perfection herself. Her golden hair was flashing in the morning sun, her features looked as if they came from a classic painting, and her lean body moved with a grace and confidence that seemed familiar. I glanced over at Tilda with an eyebrow raised.

"Werewolf," she mouthed silently.

That explained it.

"I am here for personal reasons, not in an official capacity."

Her eyes narrowed. "Really, Conall, I thought you had finished making your way through the covens." She sniffed derisively at me. "Or is this one new?"

Conall's grip on my hand tightened. "Sadie is my Destined Beloved."

The woman stopped in stunned silence and then started laughing, not a ladylike chuckle, this was a full-on, bending over at the waist, belly laugh. "You're claiming a Destined Beloved prophecy," she gasped. "That's the funniest thing I've ever heard. You can't be serious."

Conall stayed silent, his thumb stroking my hand as if he knew how much on edge I was.

The woman straightened up, wiping the tears from her face and peered over at him, taking in his calm countenance. "You're serious?"

"Yes, Detective Hanlon, I'm very serious."

Detective Hanlon studied me carefully before turning to Conall, all signs of hilarity now gone. "Very well, Conall. Why did you feel it was necessary to call in a deputy, despite your suspension and lack of power to do so?"

"I contacted Deputy Iversen as a private citizen to report

that there had been a threatening message left on Sadie's house."

Detective Hanlon's attention swung back to me. "And you would be Sadie?"

"Yes," I replied, trying very hard not to nervously fidget under her intense gaze. "Sadie Goodwin, this is my aunt's house and I'm renting it from her."

"You live here alone?"

I nodded as I wondered whether that question was relevant to the investigation or was for her personal interest. By the way she kept glancing at Conall, I had a sinking feeling that I had run into another part of his past.

"When did you discover the writing?"

"I didn't," I said. "Tilda showed it to me."

Detective Hanlon smiled and, in that moment, I could almost see the wolf she was capable of turning into. "Ah yes, Tilda Atwill. It has been a while."

I could tell from Tilda's expression that it hadn't been long enough.

"What were you doing here?" asked the detective.

Tilda lifted her head up. "I was driving past on my way to work and saw the writing. I stopped to make sure Sadie was okay."

"And who is Sadie to you?"

Tilda straightened. "She's my friend. She's also the coven leader's niece."

It sounded like there was a warning in that statement. I had a feeling that if there was, Detective Hanlon would be happy to ignore it.

"Aah, that explains a lot," she mused, and I could feel Conall stiffen beside me.

Now it was my thumb stroking his hand, hoping that it would calm him.

"Is there a point to this?" Conall said harshly. "In case

you've missed it, that warning is painted in blood, the day after a woman from this town has been viciously murdered. I would suggest you start doing what the clan leader brought you into town to do, and that is catch the killer before they target someone else."

"You are not in charge here," Detective Hanlon hissed.

Conall stepped forward, and I could see that despite her bravado, Detective Hanlon looked unsure of herself. "Regardless of what the alpha believes, I was voted in sheriff of this town, and I am still the sheriff. Do not mistake my willingness to step back for the sake of transparency as me stepping down from that position. You have been brought in to ensure that the Path Coven and the werewolf clan are fully satisfied with the perception of fairness, but the second I see you botching this investigation is the second you get kicked out of this town and I take over again. I don't care who put you here. Do you understand me?"

There was an awkward silence that nobody was willing to break as we all waited for her response.

She dipped her head. "Of course, Sheriff." She walked away to meet up with Karl who was talking to some more deputies who had turned up.

"Man, that was hot," murmured Tilda.

Conall dropped his head. "Really? That's your reaction to this situation?"

"Well, no, but I've been waiting for someone to shut that woman down for my entire life. To be able to witness it, that's made my day."

"As long as somebody is happy," he grumbled. He brought up my hand again and kissed it. "Are you okay?"

I shook my head. "No, I'm not okay. Somebody has threatened me with a message written in blood, and I'm supposed to trust in that woman when she clearly has some kind of grudge against me and you, probably mostly you."

Conall gathered me close. "Nothing is going to happen to you, I promise. I may not technically be involved in this investigation, but I am not sitting back and waiting this one out." He dropped his head and looked me in the eyes. "Do you trust me?"

"I don't know you," I whispered desperately.

"I know this situation is messed up, but I need to know how you truly feel. Do you trust me?"

Against all reason I nodded my head.

"Good, stay here and I'll be back in a few minutes."

I watched him walk towards the group of deputies who were listening to the detective with barely concealed contempt.

"Come with me." Tilda grabbed my arm and walked me a couple of steps away. She turned us so our backs were to the police. She started rubbing my back as if comforting me, while she surreptitiously pulled out her cone of silence stone from her pocket. "Okay, we can talk now. There are some things you need to know before this situation goes much further."

"Are you going to tell me that Conall had a thing going with the detective back in high school? Don't bother because I already worked that out."

"Oh, if it was only that simple," Tilda said dramatically. "Her name is Brigitte Hanlon and her father is the beta of the werewolf clan. She is the strongest female in the clan, only outranked by her father, the alpha and four of his five sons."

"Because Conall until recently was ranked near the bottom with the kids," I supplied.

"Good to know you're paying attention." Tilda glanced up nervously at the group of deputies as they started moving around the house. "She was nuts over Conall in high school and they got involved, but she's also ambitious. She knew there was no chance of him being alpha, so she moved on to his brother."

I could feel my lip curl. "Which one?"

"Almost all of them."

"Well, that's slightly distasteful."

"She went through all the brothers except Eamon, who wouldn't touch her with a ten-foot pole, but everyone knew that she had a thing for Conall. She probably would have stuck with him except for the whole..." Tilda lowered her voice which seemed weird when nobody else could hear us, "not being able to change thing."

I was still not used to the way people spoke about Conall's inability to change into a wolf as if it was some shameful condition.

"When Conall disappeared after graduation, she kind of had a meltdown. Her parents got her out of town before she could do too much damage to her chances of being the alpha wife. A couple of years ago she came back to visit and we found out she was an investigator for the state police specializing in paranormal communities." Tilda frowned. "I don't understand why she is here."

At last some information I could give her. "The council asked Conall to step down from the murder investigation, and they must have got her in to replace him."

"Why would they do that?" she asked.

"Because the victim is Jeanette Hocking."

"Oh, that's bad."

"Very," I agreed. "Is there anything else I need to be aware of?"

Tilda paused as if she was thinking hard. "No, that pretty much covers it. I just thought you'd want to know why she's looking at you like you went and stole her favorite toy, because you kinda did."

We were interrupted by Karl who stepped into our

bubble with a furious look on his face. "Are you out of your mind?" he snarled. "You can't go using a privacy spell at an active crime scene. You may as well save us some time and write your name at the top of the suspect list."

Tilda rubbed her hand over the stone and slipped it back into her pocket. Not for the first time I made a note to get Flora to teach me how to create one of them.

"I don't know what you're talking about, Deputy," she said with a forced cheerfulness. "Anyway, you just know Sadie is already at the top of that list simply because the sheriff was holding her hand."

Karl grunted and glanced at the house. "She wants to speak to you, Sadie, and she's going to have you fully scanned."

I put up my hands and took a step back. "What does that mean?"

"It means Deputies Beastpike and Karalis will check you for forensic evidence, and Deputy Greensmith will be doing a truth scan on you while answering questions."

I swallowed nervously. That did not sound good. I had too many secrets to face a truth scan with confidence. I saw Tilda fiddling in her pocket again and knew she'd activated the stone.

"Jim Greensmith is a witch from our coven. He is good at truth scans but not perfect. Stick as much to the truth as possible, but if anything comes up and you have to deviate, keep it vague. It's harder for him to pin down if the answer isn't absolute."

I could hear Karl groan. "My life used to be so much easier. Nothing good ever comes from being involved with the coven."

don't think there was any way to describe how truly uncomfortable I felt sitting next to Conall, as I was about to be interrogated by his ex-girlfriend, with a walking lie-detector in the room. I had already gone through the humiliating process of having the forensics team trawling through my belongings as if they were going to find a bowl full of blood tucked away in my lingerie drawer. Deputy Beastpike had crawled through my new home looking for evidence, and I had to keep reminding myself that I had only lived in this house for a few days. The slightly judgmental expression on his face as he crawled out from under the bed covered in dust had nothing to do with me. Although, it was a good reminder that I should give the house a good cleaning very soon. Deputy Kalaris was a little more sensitive to my situation. Either that or she was more aware of the way Conall glared at her while she was taking my fingerprints and DNA to supposedly eliminate me from the line of inquiry. I had dealt with these intrusions in my life with a sense of calm, knowing the true test was coming up.

I'd met a few members of the coven during my previous

visit to Walker Bay. Deputy Jim Greensmith had not been one of them, and I was pretty sure I would have remembered him. At first glance he wasn't overly memorable except for one feature, his hair which I was assuming was not regulation, would have reached his shoulders if it had not been caught up in a leather cord at the nape of his neck. That hair was a gorgeous range of blond hues that I found mesmerizing. I must have been staring at it overly long because it took Detective Hanlon clearing her throat for me to drag my attention back to where it was supposed to be.

"Are you ready to begin?"

I swallowed nervously and nodded as I hoped that Flora knew what she was talking about when she said that curse-breakers could fool a truth scan. Conall squeezed my knee and I smiled gratefully at him. I could count on one hand the number of people I felt would be there for me if I got in trouble. This man was proving to be one of them.

"I think we'll start at the beginning. Why are you in Walker Bay?"

"Wait a minute," Conall interrupted. "What has that got to do with her being threatened last night?"

There was that smile again. One question in and I had a very bad feeling that I was being set up for something.

"That message on her house clearly indicates that she may be part of the murder investigation. There must be a reason for that, so background information is necessary. You should know that better than anyone, Conall."

She said it with such sincerity I almost believed her. From the tension that was radiating from Conall, I could tell that he didn't. I patted his arm. "It's okay." I wasn't really sure if I was providing him with assurance or myself. Inside, I was terrified. Even though Detective Hanlon was not the magister, I knew without a doubt that if I slipped up today she would be thrilled to share the information with the Conclave.

I gave a small smile as I tried to hide my fears. "A few weeks ago I discovered that my aunt was ill. Friends of hers requested that I come to Walker Bay to see if I could help. They felt it was important for family to be close to assist in the healing process." I waited to see how Deputy Greensmith responded to that interpretation of the truth. I could hardly admit that I was kidnapped and taken across state lines in the trunk of a car. When he didn't pronounce me a liar, I continued the story that Flora and I had concocted. "I stayed for a few days until Flora recovered, and then she asked that I move to Walker Bay to be her apprentice. I agreed, but needed to go home to pack things up. I moved back here a few days ago."

"Aren't you a little bit old to be an apprentice?" Detective Hanlon asked snidely.

"I was raised outside the paranormal community by my mother who was not a witch. It has meant that my development has been delayed. By apprenticing me, Flora hopes that we will be able to combat that disadvantage."

"And who would your father be?"

I fought my lifelong inclination to shrug carelessly. "What does that possibly have to do with the fact that somebody painted my house with blood?"

I was given an insincere smile. "An investigation requires background information."

I struggled to contain my irritation. "The background information is this. I was raised by my mother after my father bolted pretty much straight after conception. As a result, I am starting my apprenticeship now. All I've done since coming to this town is try to be there for my aunt during her illness. I haven't done anything to warrant a threat against my life." I stopped speaking and tried to get control of my breathing again. From the way that Deputy Greensmith's brow was furrowed, I could tell he was having a little trouble reading me. I silently thanked Tilda on her advice. If I could just keep things vague, I might get through this without anyone thinking there was anything amiss with me.

"Did you know Jeanette Hocking?" asked Detective Hanlon.

I shook my head. "I met her the night before she was killed, at a local bar."

"And what were you doing there?"

"I was out with friends."

"I understand you had words with Miss Hocking."

Now how on Earth had she got that information so quickly? "I don't think I said anything to Miss Hocking." I tried to remember that night, but I was pretty sure that Tilda had done most of the talking.

"Yet witnesses claim that they saw you and your friends about to start a bar brawl with a woman who ended up brutally murdered within twelve hours of your confrontation." Detective Hanlon settled back in her chair, a smug look on her face.

"And your point is?" I could feel the tension radiating from Conall as he barked at the detective. "Do you really think that someone who has only just moved to this town would randomly murder a woman she barely knows, and then paint a threat on her house with blood, all within three days of returning to town?"

When put like that, it did sound faintly ridiculous.

"Jealousy makes people do strange things, you should know that better than anyone else," Detective Hanlon said calmly, despite her eyes sparking with some indefinable emotion.

"She has no reason to be jealous. She's my Destined Beloved. There will never be anyone else for me."

That did not sound like a man who was going to take things slowly, and from the expression on the detective's face, I had a very bad feeling that he had just painted a bright red target on me.

"I had no reason to wish Jeanette Hocking any harm," I said firmly. "And I had even less reason to write a threatening message on my own house." I placed a hand on Conall's knee and squeezed when I felt the tension in him, hoping he could read the non-verbal message to stand down and not make this situation worse than it already was. I knew he wanted to help, but I had met people like Brigitte Hanlon before. She had an ulterior motive to her questions, and I could see she was trying to establish a form of dominance over me. I was not going to play that game with anyone, especially not a female werewolf on a jealous power trip.

"I think that's enough for today."

I was surprised to hear a new voice entering the discussion and looked up to find an older gentleman had entered my house. Dressed in a rumpled coat with a skewed tie and messy hair, he looked like he'd put less effort into his morning look than I had.

"She's a witness," sneered Detective Hanlon, obviously not impressed by the less than elegantly dressed man standing in my living room.

"And yet you are treating her like a suspect." His eyes gentled as they glanced at me. "I'm Tarquin Burroughs, your Advocate."

I had no idea what he was talking about, but the questioning had stopped, so I was more than happy to go with whatever he said. He passed a card to the fuming detective. "Any more questions for Ms Goodwin will now be going through me. You are not to harass her in any way."

"I have been given the authority to investigate this case vigorously," the detective maintained, her eyes flashing with anger.

"Please, Detective Hanlon, we're all adults here. There is no need to pretend that your appointment is anything other than werewolf politics at its most grubby."

I could feel a smile stealing across my face. I liked this man.

Detective Hanlon narrowed her eyes. She obviously didn't. "I would suggest not flinging around unfounded accusations."

Tarquin smiled, and I was surprised and slightly perturbed to see pointed teeth in his mouth. "Aidan Tolan and I have been playing this game since before you were born. I'm sure he won't be surprised when you report back to him."

Everyone in the room could tell from the look on the detective's face that she was not happy with the direction the interrogation had taken, and we all knew that despite Detective Hanlon claiming she had been interviewing a victim, it had been an interrogation.

"This isn't finished," she snarled as she stood up.

"Of course, it isn't," Tarquin replied smoothly. "But the next time you feel a need to look in the direction of my client, I expect you to contact me instead. Believe me when I say it will save you a heap of trouble and a mountain of paperwork." He lowered his voice. "In your report to Aidan, you might want to let him know that the sheriff and Ms Goodwin are fully supported by the coven. I would suggest you be very sure before you come after them again."

You would think after that statement that Detective Hanlon would direct all her anger at Tarquin. Unfortunately, I was the one she focused her hate-filled gaze on. I could feel the way Conall vibrated with tension, and I knew this situation needed to be brought to a close before it deteriorated any further. As it was, the poor deputy looked like he wanted to be anywhere else rather than this room. I had been a witness to what happened when the berserker sheriff thought there was a threat to me. I was pretty sure that a jealous female werewolf, desperate to lock me up, would constitute a threat in his mind.

As if she was slowly coming to the realization about how close she was to being torn apart, Detective Hanlon put a forced smile on her face. "Of course, I will be in touch."

She swept from the room and I let out a breath that I had been holding. Deputy Greensmith threw an apologetic look in our direction before following the detective out the door.

Tarquin Burroughs clapped his hands together. "Well, that was fun."

"Who are you?" I couldn't help the words that came out of my mouth. I appreciated what he had done, but I had no idea who this man was, and I generally find that most favors came with a price.

Tarquin pulled out a card and passed it to me with a dramatic flourish. "I am the advocate for the Walker Bay Coven. I am here to protect your legal interests. If that woman comes within a hundred feet of you, I want you to call me immediately." With that he was gone again, like a whirlwind of energy.

I peered over at Conall. He was watching me carefully and it was making me nervous.

"Is something wrong?" I asked tentatively.

"Jim Greensmith is damn good at his job. He may not be a magister, but he can usually detect when somebody is lying in a heartbeat. You were able to tap dance around the truth and he didn't flinch. Would you mind telling me how you managed to pull that off?"

I opened my mouth and then closed it again. I honestly

had no idea what to say. If it was anyone else, I would have continued the lie but, according to the Seer, this was my Destined Beloved and he owned a part of my soul. I may not fully understand what that meant, but somewhere inside me was the realization that I couldn't taint what was happening between us with a lie.

"I can't tell you," I admitted simply. I held up my hand as I could see him about to argue. "Please understand, I barely know you, and there are things that I am not yet ready to share just as I'm sure there are things you are not ready to tell me. I won't lie to you, but I'm just not in a place where I can trust you with certain parts of my life."

I hated the hurt that flashed through his eyes.

"The one thing I've learned about secrets is they always come out sooner or later," he said as he stood up. "When that day comes, you generally need somebody who knows all the details and has your back. I want to be that person for you."

He pulled open the front door forcefully just as Tilda and Flora were about to knock.

"Sorry, ladies," he mumbled as he jammed his hat on his head and stalked past them.

Tilda looked over at me and raised an eyebrow. "First lover's quarrel?"

"We'd have to actually be lovers for that to qualify." I said as I flopped back on the couch, my hand covering my eyes.

I felt someone sit next to me and an arm go around my shoulders. I pulled my hand away to find Flora watching me carefully, her eyes full of sympathy.

"It will all work out."

I liked her optimism, but I had my doubts.

16

*W*ithin half an hour, I was at the diner having breakfast with Tilda. Flora had shooed us out of the house, assuring me that threats in blood came under the landlord's purview. I couldn't remember any of my other landlords who would have thought that.

"So, what's the problem with the sheriff?" Tilda asked as we waited for the food.

"This whole Destined Beloved thing is hard," I complained. "I don't know this person and yet I'm supposed to believe that we're soul mates." I waved a fork in the air. "People think it would be so much easier to just know who their soul mate is. It isn't. I'm not ready to trust my deepest, darkest secrets to a man I've barely spoken to a handful of times. Do I tell him about past boyfriends? Do I ask him for a list of his past girlfriends?"

"You don't have to ask, just get the yearbook from the high school for the year when he graduated. That will cover most of the list."

"Well that's just super, isn't it?" There was no way I could stop the sarcasm. "You know, if I'd been given a choice, I'd go with a socially awkward accountant who thinks a wild time is a Star Trek convention."

"Wow," Tilda said, her food forgotten. "Someone really did a number on you, didn't they?"

"Yes, they did, and before you ask, I'm not ready to tell you those kinds of details yet, but my Destined Beloved seems to think that I should tell him everything."

I looked up as the waitress dropped our food in front of us.

"He is kind of intense," Tilda agreed. "But I'm pretty sure he's going to be worth the effort. Maybe he's accepting this whole Destined Beloved thing faster than you."

"Maybe, but he needs to calm down a bit. I thought he was going to rip the detective to pieces. If it hadn't been for the advocate turning up, I have a feeling things would have gone downhill fast." I peered over at Tilda. "I'm assuming that an advocate is a lawyer."

Tilda nodded "He might not look like much, but Tarquin's the best advocate in the state, and he is totally loyal to the coven. As soon as I called Flora about what happened, she contacted him. He came straight over. You couldn't get anyone better," she assured me.

"He certainly shut down Detective Hanlon pretty quickly." I frowned as I remembered a slight anomaly to my protector's appearance. "By the way, what kind of witch has those weird teeth?" I asked.

"Oh, Tarquin isn't a witch, he's a vampire. He just does work for the coven when we need it," Tilda said as she calmly shoved my world off its axis.

"My lawyer is a vampire," I said slowly. "Somehow that seems kind of wrong, like I shouldn't be surprised, but I am."

"I know, the whole vampire and lawyer blood sucker thing just seems a little stereotypical, but he's a really good advocate."

"But he's a vampire," I repeated, unsure of where I was going with this.

Tilda waved her hand in the air. "Don't worry, just because he's a vampire doesn't make him dangerous."

"Everything I've heard about vampires makes me pretty confident that they are dangerous."

Tilda straightened in her seat. "Vampires are like normal people, some of them are gentle as lambs, and some of them will rip your throat out. You can't judge a whole species based on the worst of them."

"So, where does my lawyer land on that spectrum?" I asked, not entirely sure I wanted the answer.

"It depends on what kind of day he's having."

Well, wasn't that comforting?

"He's really okay," Tilda assured me. "The vampire nest in Walker Bay is pretty elitist and Tarquin doesn't quite fit in. He had a great-grandmother who was a witch, so we were able to adopt him into the coven, like the sheriff except there's no prophecy involved, and there's no conspiracy to get him kicked out of his job."

"Do you really think the members of the werewolf clan wants to replace Conall?" I asked.

"I would say most of the werewolves are happy with him, but Aidan Tolan's feelings for his son define dysfunctional." Tilda replied. "With the other coven supporting him, things could get messy."

"Why do you call it 'the other coven'? I've also heard some people call it the Path Coven. Which is it?"

Tilda frowned. "I'm sorry, sometimes I forget this is all new to you. A lot of the things we say must be really confusing, I'll try to do better. Covens are generally named after the town they're in. Walker Bay Coven is from Walker Bay. Sometimes we're not very imaginative, but at least everyone knows where we stand."

"So, no Blood Moon Rising Coven?"

Tilda chuckled. "No, but that would be a cool name. Problems come up when a splinter coven breaks off from the main one, and Walker Bay has one of the biggest of those splinter covens. Not long after they split from the main coven, they started communicating with other splinter covens, and next thing we have this worldwide movement and they're all calling themselves collectively The Path." Tilda rolled her eyes, disdain dripping from her voice. "I personally think it's a cult, but a lot of other witches are losing their minds over them. They've got weird rules like they will only accept female practicing witches. All the boys get tossed out when they turn fourteen."

I was horrified. "Why would they do that to their children?"

"Because they're a cult," Tilda replied as if I should have already accepted this.

"What happens to the boys?"

"We take them in. A lot of the families foster the boys until they're ready to make a decision about their future. Most of them end up in our coven. Jim Greensmith's part of our coven, and his mother is one of the Path coven leaders."

"Like Jeanette and Myra?" I queried.

"Yes, Jim's mom is Elspeth Pickering. She only had the one child so in her mind she was barren as she never had a daughter."

My face wrinkled in distaste as I felt sympathy for the man who not long ago was scanning me for lies. "That's pretty reprehensible."

"Sounds like standard practice for a cult," Tilda said sagely. "Some people have caught on and call them the Path Coven. Those of us with a little less respect still call them the other coven."

"And they hate the Walker Bay Coven?" I queried.

Tilda tilted her head to the side. "I think hate may be too strong a word. There is some animosity because they believe that Flora is not a legitimate coven leader. They believe that the Seer shouldn't have got involved, and that the position should have gone to her older sister who had been training for it her whole life."

"But Collette left town," I was trying to remember as much of the story as I had been told. "Shouldn't that have ended the feud?"

Tilda sighed. "You'd think so, but there is one thing you need to learn about witches, we can carry grudges like nobody else, even when everybody has forgotten the original grievance. This situation is partially a result of that character flaw."

"Why are they so desperate to prevent Conall from investigating Jeanette's death," I asked quietly.

Tilda shrugged. "I don't know. This whole complaint that there was bad blood between them is ridiculous. Conall never cared enough about her for there to be a problem. Unfortunately, the werewolf clan has a lot of influence in this town. Not many people want to go up against them, especially when they've got the backing of some malcontent witches."

"So, we just wait for her to solve the case." I was determined to see a positive way out of this situation.

"If she solves it," Tilda said glumly.

I paused my eating. "You don't think she'll solve it?"

"Think about it. Brigitte Hanlon is completely under the control of the werewolf alpha, who has made no secret that he wants the sheriff out. What better way is there to do that than to have an unsolved murder hanging over his head where he was considered a person of interest?"

"That's not fair."

Tilda gave me a look as if she found my naive view of the

world to be both charming and irritating. "What about this mess makes you think anyone is playing fair?"

I pushed away my plate as my appetite fled. "I hate politics."

"You're preaching to the choir," Tilda said as she wiped her hands with a napkin. "Unfortunately, my grandmother has a tendency to jump into political messes and drags me with her."

I grimaced. "That's going to happen to me too, isn't it?"

"With Flora being your aunt, you better believe it."

"Allegedly my aunt," I mumbled, wondering if at any point we would confirm scientifically what the magic users in this town were now spouting as fact.

Tilda frowned at me. "I know you aren't used to this, but if Flora said that you are Jasper's daughter then that is what you are. Constantly doubting it isn't going to make it go away." She watched me carefully. "Have you been having any success with training with Flora? Maybe when we find your magic ability, you'll feel a bit more confident."

"Not really." I didn't have the heart to tell the person who was quickly becoming the closest thing I had to a friend that we already knew my magical ability, and I would never be able to tell her what it was because it had put a death sentence over my head.

I looked at the clock on the wall. "We had better get to work before people start complaining."

Tilda pushed the last of her meal in her mouth. "Sure, although I don't know what your hurry is. I'm self-employed, and you've shut the library and can work at your leisure. It isn't like we have anybody to answer to if we're a little late."

"Doesn't mean we can slack off," I replied as I stood up.

"Great, you're one of those people," Tilda complained as she followed me out of the diner.

"What do you mean, those people?"

"I think the word my grandmother used to use on reports was conscientious."

I couldn't help the smile that crossed my face. "I got that on a lot of my reports."

"Of course, you did."

ot long after starting my hunt through the magical texts in the Walker Bay coven library I realized that what was most needed was a searchable computer database. The problem with books which had been handed down through the generations was that there was no logic behind how the spells had been written down. A love spell could just as easily be followed by a fertility spell or one for treating some strange rash. I could see a discussion about bringing computers into the library was going to feature strongly in my next discussion with Flora. Considering the most modern thing I'd found was a phone that looked like it was installed in the early twentieth century, I didn't like my chances. With a sigh, I settled in and started working my way through the mountain of books that I had found hidden in the back room. The hunt for curses hidden among the hundreds of grimoires in the library was a slow and tedious one. I rubbed the back of my neck trying to alleviate the pain that was settling there. Being hunched over a table filled with books had caused the muscles in my back to start complaining loudly.

"You look like you need a break."

I glanced up to discover Tilda had managed to find her way into the library without me noticing. She was looking around as if she thought she shouldn't be in here. The previous librarian had instituted a ruling that only the most experienced witches were able to access the coven library. With Flora's support I had expanded the number of witches who could now walk in here. Some had no issue with the new rules. Some, like Tilda, still looked guilty every time they stepped through the doorway. "You finished already?"

Tilda snorted. "What do you mean, already? You've been at this for ages."

I squinted at the clock on the wall. No wonder I was feeling sore, I'd barely moved in five hours. I tilted my head to the side and felt a crack. "What are you doing here? Shouldn't you still be working?"

Tilda ran her hands across several books on a shelf. "I finished my deliveries and wondered whether you wanted a ride home. I dropped you off here remember."

I looked over at the pile of books I'd barely made a dent in.

"I should probably keep going," I said half-heartedly.

Tilda watched me carefully. "You look wrecked, what are you doing here anyway?"

"I'm cataloging all the spells in the books and trying to work out an easier way to access the information," I replied trying my best not to lie to my new friend. "I think I need to talk to Flora about bringing in some computers."

Tilda stilled. "Oh, that would not be a popular move."

"Why not? There is no logic to the information in these books. If we don't put a better system in place, a lot of this knowledge is going to be lost, simply because nobody will know it is in here."

Tilda held her hands up. "I'm not your enemy on this one.

Your enemy consists of the people who almost tore the meeting hall down when it was suggested that someone type up the meeting notes rather than write them by hand in a leather-bound journal." She grimaced at what was obviously a painful memory.

I contemplated that statement and then shrugged. I was going to drag this library into the twenty-first century no matter what the coven said. Just a day of looking through these beautiful old books had convinced me that the knowledge in this building was far too precious to let it vanish, despite a community too caught up in the past to realize what they could lose.

"So, do you want that ride?" asked Tilda.

With a last look around the room I nodded. Tomorrow would be soon enough to tackle this problem.

When we pulled up at the house, I was pleased to see that there was no longer any sign of the threat from the night before.

"Looks like Flora managed to get it cleaned up," Tilda commented.

"I'm just hoping that it isn't going to be a standard wake up call," I replied.

Tilda glanced over at me, a sympathetic expression on her face. "Do you need company?"

I shook my head. "I'll be fine."

"If you're sure…"

I squared my shoulders and tried to project a confidence I didn't really feel. "I'm going to make sure all my doors and windows are locked. I'll also see if I need to replace any of them." I smiled weakly. "If there is a problem, I'm pretty sure the sheriff will come riding to my rescue."

Tilda chuckled. "Just make sure you call him before things go too bad. For all of our sakes."

I watched her drive away, struggling with the temptation

to call her back. I fought the unfamiliar feeling. After having to rely on myself for so long, being thrust into a community of people who seemed to care about my well-being was, to be perfectly honest, really weird. It was also kind of nice. I couldn't help the slight smile that crossed my face when I walked up to my front door. When I got closer, I noticed a piece of paper stuck to the door. As I scanned the note I could feel myself frowning. It seemed that Flora had not only organized to have the wall cleaned, but she had also put up some wards to provide protection from any intruders so I would feel safe sleeping at night. Considering we already believed that this house had a curse on it, I wasn't sure that adding more spells to the mix wasn't going to cause issues. I screwed up the note and opened the door, hoping that her actions didn't react with what was already in the house, like mixing too many chemicals together. I closed the door behind me and turned around, a small scream coming out of me when I saw what was in the middle of my living room.

I truly believed that I was getting better at dealing with the unexpected in the short amount of time that I had been in Walker Bay. I had dealt with a centaur being my doctor, my future partner being dictated by a Seer, said future partner being a berserker. None of that had disturbed me as much as seeing what looked like a life-size crystal statue in my house. I waved my hand in front of the glass at the person encased inside.

"Myra, are you in there?"

I didn't know what I was hoping for. At this stage I would have been thrilled with a blink, but there was nothing. I knew I should be wondering why Myra was in my house. I had a feeling that I was not going to like the answer to that question, but at this moment I was more concerned with how I was going to get her out of her crystal prison. I needed

Flora. I started searching through my bag for my phone, irritation surging through me when I couldn't find it.

I spun around when I heard the front door open. This was not a sight I wanted to share with anyone.

"You left your phone in the car, it must have fallen out of your...Oh, wow."

Thank goodness it was Tilda. I had no idea how I was going to explain this situation to anyone else.

"That's not what I was expecting when I walked into your house." Tilda's eyes were glued to the scene in front of her, much like mine were. "What happened?"

I waved at the frozen statue in front of me. "It seems that Flora put some protection wards up when she was organizing the cleaning of my wall."

Tilda flinched. "The wards of a coven leader shielding her family would be strong. They get an extra kick from the protectiveness she feels for you."

"It seems so because now I have a witchcicle in my living room and I'm trying to work out what the next step is."

Tilda walked around Myra, studying her thoughtfully. "You know, there is a whole stream of psychology that believes that you can tell a witch's emotional state from the spells they cast." I flinched as she tapped on the frozen statue in my living room and a hollow sound rang through my house. "If that's true I'm seeing a whole lot of controlled rage in this spell. It looks like Flora was good and mad about somebody threatening you."

I grabbed my phone out of her hand. "Warm and fuzzy as that sentiment is, we need to get this spell lifted or there is going to be hell to pay."

"What are you doing?" asked Tilda, still staring at my unfortunate art piece.

"I'm calling Flora to come back here and reverse this spell."

Tilda snatched my phone back. "Are you out of your mind? If Flora finds out that Myra broke into your house, she is going to go ballistic."

"So, what is your suggestion? That I leave Myra here as an interesting talking point at my first dinner party."

Tilda glanced meaningfully at the house which looked like it was inching closer to being condemned with every door you opened. "I don't think you'll be having dinner parties any time soon."

I was strangely insulted on behalf of the house I was beginning to grow fond of, and held out my hand. "I need Flora to fix this. That means I need my phone."

Tilda held the phone behind her back, and I had a bad feeling that I was going to need to tackle her before I could retrieve it. "Whatever you do, you cannot tell Flora that Myra broke into your house."

I put my hands on my hips and stared at the floor, wondering when my life had become so complicated. "I know she won't be happy, but if I call her, she can lift the protection booby traps, yell at Myra a bit, and then we can go about our normal lives."

Tilda shook her head. "That's a very nice fantasy, but it isn't the way that this situation is going to play out. Myra hasn't just broken into your house. She has broken into the house of the niece of the rightful coven leader of Walker Bay. That action alone could trigger massive political repercussions for the witch population in this town. Despite what the Path Coven say about their legitimacy, their existence is barely tolerated by the Walker Bay Coven, and that's mostly based on Flora's good will. She will see this action by Myra as a direct threat to her leadership and may respond in kind."

"So, what do I do?" Nothing in my life had prepared me for any of this.

"You have to break the spell yourself, and we need to put

a control on Myra before this situation blows completely out of proportion."

I chewed my bottom lip. "I'm seeing a problem with that plan."

Tilda smiled and placed her a comforting hand on my arm. "I know you don't think you have any magical abilities. When Flora set up the wards, she would have allowed a back door into it so you would be able to break it. The thing you need to remember about magic is it isn't usually a solo act. I'll guide the spell, but I'll need you to join me."

That didn't sound too hard. I shook my hands. "What do you want me to do?"

Tilda took hold of my hand and pulled me to stand closer to Myra. "Put your other hand on the statue thing," she ordered as she placed her free hand against the casing.

I copied her actions hesitantly.

"Now, I need you to close your eyes and focus your energy through your hands, both towards me and Myra."

I took in a breath and tried to focus.

"You need to focus harder," grumbled Tilda. "I'm not getting anything from you."

I nodded as I tried to concentrate. Until a month ago I had no idea that there was a world of magic existing within a world of celebrities and smartphones. That is the world I grew up in, and that upbringing meant that I felt slightly ridiculous standing here, holding hands with a witch, believing that some power was going to surge through me. The other times I had used my ability as a cursebreaker had been natural and intuitive. What we were doing here felt stupid, like we were little kids who had watched too many superhero movies.

Tilda pulled her hand away from mine. "This isn't working."

I stayed silent. I knew it wasn't working because of me.

Whether it was because of my mindset, or because I was simply unable to wield magic except when it came to my curse breaking ability, I truly didn't know. I did, however, feel slightly inadequate. A sudden thought struck me.

"Is she aware of what we're doing?" I waved my hand in front of Myra's face, looking for some reaction.

Tilda slapped my hand away. "Not really. The crystal acts like a barrier. At best she can see black shapes, but she can't hear us or communicate with us in any way."

That was good. The last thing I wanted was for Myra to become aware of how truly incompetent I was. I frowned as I heard a phone ringing from Tilda's bag. "Shouldn't you answer that?"

Tilda shook her head. "We need to do this now," she said with a new determination as she grabbed both my hands and placed them against the crystal, her own hands covering them. "Now, I need you to concentrate and reach inside yourself. The magic is there, you just need to be willing to use it."

I took a deep breath and tried to empty my mind of all the fears and doubts that were running through it. I knew I had magic. I'd already proved it when I broke the curse that had held my aunt captive. I just needed to tap into that power and push it through Tilda. I took a deep breath and emptied my mind. Rather than focusing like Tilda was telling me, I let my mind soar free. It was like I was a balloon that was floating away, buffeted by wind currents. In the distance I could see something. I wasn't sure what it was, but I knew that I needed to follow it. As I got closer, an indefinable shape seemed to reach out to me, and I felt a warmth and strength surge through me.

"You're getting there," Tilda murmured as I felt the warmth flow through my limbs. I opened my eyes, wanting to know if I could see what I was feeling as it flowed out of my hands. I felt strong and at peace in a way that I'd never known in my life.

Tilda frowned. "There's a strange energy to your magic. I've never felt anything like it before."

I was jolted by her statement. That wasn't good. The last thing I needed was for Tilda to realize that there was something different about the way I wielded magic. Fortunately, the moment was interrupted with a sharp cracking noise. I snatched my hands back as the casing around Myra began to fall away. As the last pieces hit the ground, there was a small moan from Myra, and she started to topple. Both Tilda and I caught her before she hit the ground.

"What happened?" she groaned.

etween the two of us, Tilda and I managed to help a disoriented Myra to the couch and set her down relatively gently.

"What am I doing here? What have you done to me?"

Considering that she was the one in the wrong here, I was a little put out by her accusations. "I believe you broke into my house," I said with a slight bite to my tone.

Her eyes widened as she started to remember what had led to this moment.

I was about to continue questioning when Tilda's phone started insistently ringing again.

Tilda glanced at the screen and grimaced. "I have to take this," she said apologetically.

I watched as she walked to the edge of the room, her voice low.

"Do you need a drink?" I asked roughly, not entirely sure of the etiquette you were supposed to use with the person you had caught breaking into your house.

Myra nodded, her shoulders slumped as if she'd finally grasped that her decisions leading up until this point may not have been good ones. Keeping an eye on my reluctant guest as I fetched her some water, I passed her the glass and waited for Tilda to join the coming interrogation. When she came back in the room, I could tell something was wrong.

"What's happening now?" I asked.

Tilda looked down at the ground, her phone grasped in her hand. "I have to get going."

"Why?" I asked, a little incredulous that my partner in crime was choosing this moment to bail on me.

"My little sister just got asked to the prom by a werewolf and my mom is about to stroke out." She paused as I looked at her quizzically. "In her mind she's leapt straight from prom to teenage pregnancy."

Considering what I had heard about the promiscuity of werewolf males, I could understand her mom's point of view.

"You stay there," I pointed at Myra as I walked Tilda towards the door. I lowered my voice. "What am I supposed to do with her?"

Tilda sighed. "It's up to you. I know I said you couldn't tell Flora because of the possible repercussions to the covens, but the fact is she broke into your house. She cannot get away with that. You need to find out why she did this, and she needs to realize the gravity of her offense." Tilda looked me squarely in the eye. "You are the niece of the coven leader, the only family she has. I know this is all new to you and if there was a way to make this easier I would, but you need to step up and let these people know they can't push you around without consequences."

I had no idea how I was going to do that. I was a librarian for a reason. I preferred dealing with books rather than people. Taking a position of confrontation and power did not sit well with me.

Tilda put her hand on my shoulder and smiled sympathetically. "You can do this. I know you've been tossed in the deep end with everything that has happened, but you are stronger than you think you are. You just need to let yourself prove it."

With that piece of advice she turned away and left me alone with a burglar with magical powers.

I grabbed one of the mismatched chairs from the kitchen and dragged it in front of Myra. If I was going to do this interrogation alone then I wanted to have as much of a psychological advantage over her as I possibly could.

"So, did you want to explain to me why I came home to find you looking like an art piece in the middle of my living room?" I asked casually.

"I would think that had something to do with the wards you set up around this place," she replied with a sarcasm that I didn't think she was entitled to.

"You're talking about the consequence of the situation, whereas I want to know about the cause. Those wards would not have gone off unless you had broken in with ill intent. Now, I am being rather accommodating by allowing you the opportunity to explain to me what you were doing. You choose to ignore my overtures of friendship and I will be forced to contact my aunt and the sheriff. I'm guessing neither of them will be as understanding as I am."

Myra flinched at the mention of Flora and Conall, but she remained stubbornly tight-lipped. I waited, hoping that the silence would pressure her into talking, but she seemed determined to wait me out.

"I know you must be in mourning for your friend," I said gently. "Grief can sometimes make people act in bizarre ways. Usually I'm pretty understanding when it comes to those kinds of situations, but you broke into my house. I can't let that go. Whatever your motivation is, you've committed a crime, and I don't care enough about your position or reputation to keep that quiet. This is a small town.

Before the day is out, everybody is going to know what you did. Any standing that you have in this town is going to be tainted by what may have been a moment of madness. Help me understand why you did this."

When she didn't reply I glanced at my watch. I really didn't have the time or the energy for this. With a sigh I stood up. "Fine, you haven't given me any other choice." I reached over to grab my phone and started dialing the sheriff. Before I'd finished, I glanced up and froze. Despite Myra still having the same blank expression, tears were rolling silently down her face.

Great. I really didn't cope well with somebody else's tears. Normally in these circumstances I would show comfort by putting an arm around their shoulder. In this situation I didn't feel like that was the correct course of action to take. With a grimace I dropped the phone, sat down beside her and awkwardly patted her on the shoulder. A small part of me was concerned that I was being played, but there seemed to be a genuine air of misery surrounding the young woman.

"What's going on, Myra?" I asked, trying to keep the irritation at this whole situation out of my voice. "I may not know you very well, but I'm pretty sure you're acting out of character here. Despite what you may think, I'm not your enemy."

Rather than helping, my words only seemed to make her cry harder. Before I could say anything else, she dropped her head against my chest and proceeded to sob as if her heart was breaking. I tentatively patted her on the back and glanced desperately at the front door. If there was ever a time I wanted Tilda to come back, this was it. I barely knew this woman, and not only did I need to decide what to do about the whole break-in situation, I was also a witness to what I was sure was going to be considered one of the more embarrassing moments of her life. Once she pulled herself together and remembered where she was, she was going to hate that I witnessed her meltdown.

It seemed like hours before the deluge of tears began to slow down. By that time, I had given up trying to comfort her and just leaned back against the couch and waited for the storm to pass. She sat up and we both looked down at the wet patch which had spread across my chest.

"You feeling any better now?" I asked as I pulled the fabric away from my skin and tried to air it out.

Myra gave what I'm hoping was a small smile. It didn't really look like one, but I was interpreting the expression.

"You need to explain what you were doing here," I said softly. "You know I can't let this go. The second I contact Flora or the sheriff I am going to lose control of this situation. I can't emphasize enough how important it is to you that you don't force me to take that action."

Myra's shoulders slumped and I prepared myself for another round of tears. "She was my best friend," she sniffed. "I went with her mother to identify the body."

My heart went out to her. Just the basic description I had got from Karl and Conall about the murder scene was enough to tell me I would never have wanted to be in Myra's position. I reached into my purse, grabbed a tissue and passed it to her. She accepted it and I saw a flash of gratitude. I had a feeling that was all I was going to get.

"I'm sorry," I said gently. "I can't even imagine how terrible that must have been for you."

Myra nodded and her breath hitched. "Her mother is a mess. I don't even know if Ilsa is going to survive this. Jeanette was all she had, and somebody tore her apart. They destroyed her without even thinking about it."

"I understand that you are grieving, I don't understand why that grief made you break into my home."

"Because you're next," she said, echoing the message I'd

found on my house. "There has to be a reason they want to kill you as well. If I can find out why they want you dead, maybe I can find out who hurt her."

There was a part of me that knew that the message on my house could only be related to Jeanette's murder. I had managed to suppress the terror that knowledge caused throughout the day. Having Myra pronounce it in such a matter-of-fact manner brought that fear back with a vengeance.

a s Myra pulled up at the perfectly average looking house that could be found in any suburb, I recognized that those people who cared about me might not agree with some of the decisions I had been making. Let's have a recap. After finding an intruder in my home who had a definite grudge against me, I had not only failed to contact police, I had agreed to accompany the alleged criminal to get some answers about a murder victim from her boyfriend. I hadn't even insisted on driving myself, I had allowed Myra to drive us, which I was sure violated some rule about allowing a criminal to take you to a secondary location. I could give a drawn-out story to attempt to justify my thinking, but let's just go with the whole murder mystery making strange bedfellows explanation, and neither of us having any faith in Brigitte Hanlon wanting to solve the case. I had a feeling my Destined Beloved would not approve.

"Does he know we want to speak to him?" I asked nervously as I stared at the house which looked perfectly safe...or like a serial killer's lair. I'd lost the ability to differentiate between the two when I crossed over into this town.

"Maybe we should leave him be. He's probably grieving. His girlfriend was murdered a couple of days ago. Don't you think us waltzing in and demanding answers is a little insensitive?"

"Jaxon will talk to me," Myra said confidently. "When we broke up it was on good terms."

That explanation caught my attention. "Let me get this straight. Jeanette's current boyfriend is your ex-boyfriend?"

Myra waved her hand airily. "We went out for a few months, but I wouldn't really characterize it as a boyfriend situation. More as friends with benefits between real relationships."

"Did you and Jeanette have a habit of dating each other's exes?" I asked, wincing as I remembered that they had also both gone out with Conall.

"Small town living," Myra replied. "It's like a game of musical chairs. Sooner or later everyone has a go at dating everyone else."

I pondered that statement as we walked towards the front door. There was so much about this town that I still didn't understand. I really hoped that lack of knowledge wasn't going to get me in trouble.

Myra went to open the door and I held out a hand to stop her.

"What are you doing?" she asked.

"You can't just walk in there," I hissed.

Myra shook my hand off and confidently opened the door. "You are seriously going to have to loosen up if you are planning on staying with Conall," she sniffed, the disdain dripping from her voice. "Believe me when I say that if we want answers, we do not want to give Jaxon any warning that we're here. It's better that we surprise him."

I followed her into the house, hoping this wasn't another

bad decision. It took less than a minute to discover that it was.

"How could this happen?" Myra's horrified whisper echoed as if we were standing in a tomb. In a literal sense we were. We had found Jaxon McDonald slumped on the couch in the living room with a knife sticking out of his chest, the expression on his face one of surprise. I stepped around the frozen Myra and, although I could immediately tell it was a fruitless action, I checked to see if there were any signs of life.

After searching for any indication of breathing or a pulse, I looked up at Myra, sympathy slashing through me at the devastated expression on her face. "He's dead, we need to call the police."

Those words seemed to jolt Myra out of her daze. "Not yet, we need to speak to him first."

I froze, wondering whether the loss of her best friend and an ex-boyfriend were enough to cause the woman to finally snap. "He's dead," I said gently. "I don't think that talking to him is going to make a bit of difference to him now."

And there was that withering look of condescending scorn being tossed in my direction again. I should have known that the truce we seemed to have agreed to since I found Myra frozen in my living room would not last for long. Myra stepped forward and placed one hand on Jaxon's head and one just above the protruding knife.

"What...?" I stopped myself from my natural reaction to ask questions about what she was doing, knowing instinctively that my lack of knowledge about the paranormal world was not something I wanted to share with Myra.

I held up my hands. "Have at it."

I stood back and let her do what she wanted, even though I was internally wincing at the thought of Conall's reaction to the way we were messing with his crime scene. I was so enthralled by Myra's actions that it took me a couple of seconds to notice the shimmer of light that had started to develop in the corner of the room. I watched with a curious detachment as the lights coalesced into a form that resembled the man slumped on the couch, minus the knife sticking out of his chest. You would think that seeing what seemed to be a ghost appearing before my eyes would have me running for the door. The fact that I wasn't proved how much my world view had changed in the last few weeks. Unable to take my eyes away from the man that had joined us, I cleared my throat. Myra looked up and I saw her expression tighten as she dropped her hands.

"Jaxon," she breathed.

"What are you doing?" he asked, his voice seething in fury.

I could understand his anger. He had obviously died in a horrific way and then was brought back from wherever his soul was supposed to go by an ex-girlfriend who was going to demand answers. I'd be pretty ticked off too. I glanced quickly at Myra hoping she'd be able to handle him.

"Jaxon," she repeated.

Okay, so no help there.

I stepped forward. "Hi, Jaxon." I stopped moving when his attention swung to me. "We were just wondering what happened to you?" I know, as far as conversations went, it wasn't a stellar performance, but I challenge anyone to deal with this kind of situation without coming across as an idiot. From the look on Myra's face I could tell she wasn't impressed with me either.

"You want to know what happened to me?" His voice started off low but rose with each word. "Now, let's see. A couple of days ago my girlfriend was murdered. Of course, the first person the cops want to talk to is the boyfriend, because the boyfriend is always the prime suspect in a murder case. For the last two days I have dealt with people looking at me as if I'm an ax murderer. Even my own mother asked me if I did it." He thundered the last part.

"I'm sure she doesn't really think you're guilty," I offered weakly.

Jaxon glared at me. "My point is, she doesn't care if I did it or not. She just wants to know if she needs to put in place an escape plan."

I swallowed nervously. That was an interesting form of maternal devotion.

Jaxon continued his tirade. "I barely start getting my head around the fact that Jeanette was murdered when someone jumps me in my own house, and I get to follow her into the afterlife." He glared at Myra. "And then, when I finally get to the point where I think I'm at peace, my spirit gets yanked back by an ex-girlfriend who knew I never wanted to see her again."

"You don't have to be rude," Myra sniffed indignantly.

"To top it all off, I'm pretty sure that the only reason I'm sitting there with a knife in me is because my so-called loving girlfriend was cheating on me."

Both Myra and I froze.

"Jeanette was cheating on you?" I repeated slowly, wanting to be sure I had this right.

Jaxon turned in my direction. "Who are you, and what are you doing in my house?" he demanded.

Myra got to her feet. "It's okay, Jaxon," she said wearily. "She's Flora's niece. She came with me."

Jaxon swung his head in her direction. "You think that makes her being in my house alright?" he demanded. "I told you the last time that I never wanted to see you again. That doesn't change just because I'm dead."

I winced at the anger in his voice, pretty sure that message was going to be received loud and clear. For a split second I saw pain in Myra's eyes. Despite the flippant way she had described her relationship with Jaxon, I could see that her feelings had obviously run deeper than she had let on.

"Hey, there's no need to be mean."

Jaxon took another step towards me. "I have been murdered in my own home while having a beer and watching a disappointing game of baseball. If there is a time for me to be a little put out, I think this is it."

"I get it," I said. "The last few days you have been dealt a really bad hand, but Myra had nothing to do with that." I fervently hoped that Myra had nothing to do with that. "We came here to find out if there was anything different about Jeanette that you had noticed lately."

Jaxon gave out a short bark of laughter. "You mean, other than the fact she was cheating on me."

"Are you sure?" I asked. "Or is this just some suspicion you had?"

"As sure as I can be without actually seeing her do the deed," he replied.

"Do you know who it was?" I asked bluntly. I figured he was already upset with the world. Nothing else I asked was going to make the situation any worse.

Jaxon shook his head. "I wish I did. I'd have got to him before he got to me."

I had to stop myself from asking if murder was a normal way of ridding yourself of romantic rivals in this town.

"One thing I do know is the guy was strong and fast," Jaxon continued. "He would never have got me otherwise."

"Was it a witch?" Myra ventured.

Jaxon shook his head. "No, I would have felt something if magic was used. This was sheer brute force. No finesse anywhere."

"Then, how...?"

Jaxon ducked his head. I would have thought that it was impossible for a spirit to blush, but I could have sworn I saw a tinge of red on his cheeks.

"That beer I was drinking wasn't the first one I'd had. I may have been a little lax with security the last couple of days. My wards weren't as strong as they should have been, and I wasn't exactly at the top of my game."

"Oh, Jaxon," murmured Myra.

I cleared my throat. I could tell they were having a moment and I hated the idea of disturbing them, but I knew we were on a time limit. "Is there anything else you can tell us?"

Jaxon shook his head. "It happened so quick I don't have a clue who did it. I will tell you something, there was no emotion behind it. It was quick and clean. I barely felt a thing." He grimaced. "Course, that could be because of the alcohol."

I narrowed my eyes as the edges of Jaxon began to blur. I had a feeling that our time was limited. "Is there anything else that you can tell us about Jeanette," I asked urgently.

"Typical," snorted Jaxon. "Even at the scene of my brutal murder, Jeanette's still taking up all the attention."

He seemed to pause to take in a deep breath, which was all kinds of weird because everyone in the room knew that he really didn't need to do that. It seemed some habits transcended death.

Jaxon focused on Myra. "You knew Jeanette better than anyone. I was never going to be enough for her long term. Relationships for Jeanette were always transactional. She would be with somebody only if they held some value. I no longer had anything she wanted, but the fact she cheated rather than just cutting me loose tells me that the next guy may not have been completely free to take her on. If I were you, I would look at someone with a lot to lose."

I glanced over at Myra. Jaxon was now so blurred I could barely see him. Myra seemed to be waning herself as if she was using all her strength to keep him here.

"Let him go," I barked.

For a second, time was suspended as the barely there shadow of Jaxon reached out an arm as if to touch Myra's cheek. Myra reached for him but found her hand wiping through nothingness. She dropped to her knees.

I stepped towards Myra, my arm outstretched, wanting to help her with the pain.

"Don't touch me, I don't need a hug," she snapped.

I stopped my movement, raised my hands and stepped back. "Whatever you say. Is there anything you do need?"

She shook her head, her eyes glued to the ground.

"In that case we need to get out of here and call the cops."

She shook her head again, refusing to look up.

I turned and headed away from Myra and her grief. I knew once Brigitte Hanlon walked into this house, Myra would be facing a whole different kind of pain.

20

"*L*et me get this straight. You came to your ex-boyfriend's house to give condolences for his girl-friend that got murdered.

Myra nodded, her expression not changing at all.

Brigitte Hanlon tapped a manicured finger against her cheek. "That's very generous of you, especially considering it was the same girlfriend who most likely stole him from you in the first place."

Myra gave her a cold smile. "I'm evolved that way."

Just as I'd suspected, Detective Hanlon had not been happy to find another body related to her case. She was particularly annoyed that Myra and I had discovered it. Fortunately, Myra was currently fielding all questions and it seemed that she understood the very best way to get under Hanlon's skin. That must be one of the benefits of attending high school together.

Hanlon arched a perfectly shaped eyebrow. "I don't seem to remember you as being understanding when someone went out with one of your exes."

Myra gave a light laugh. "It's not like I had a meltdown,

started stalking him, and had to be sent away. I believe that was your romantic experience."

The expression on Hanlon's face was worth every uncomfortable moment I'd had to spend in Myra's company for the last couple of hours. I doubted that Myra and I would ever be friends, but I had a feeling she would make a pretty good ally, although I doubted she would be interested in the position.

Obviously, my face gave away my enjoyment at Detective Hanlon's predicament, because she gave up baiting Myra and decided to turn her attention to me.

"I'm quite surprised to find you being so friendly with one of your boyfriend's old flings," she sneered

No more than I was. "I'm pretty evolved myself."

Next to me Myra snorted, and Hanlon's attention immediately swung back to her.

"Do you find this situation funny?" Hanlon barked.

"No, but I find you attempting to be something you're not completely hilarious," Myra shot back. "Nobody in this town has any faith that you have a clue what you're doing. I could do better at solving Jeanette's murder." She jerked a thumb in my direction. "Even this one could do better."

I wasn't even going to try to twist that statement into a compliment. I also wasn't going to make the mistake of trying to jump between these two. My mother brought me up with a healthy sense of self-preservation, and I could tell these two women were seconds from throwing down. As a police officer, I would assume that Hanlon might have the training to win any fight that broke out, but I had a sneaking suspicion that Myra was working on a high dose of adrenaline and rage. There was no way I was going to make the mistake of counting her out.

Fortunately, calmer heads prevailed when a throat was

nervously cleared as the two women tried to stare each other down.

"Detective Hanlon?" Poor Deputy Greensmith looked as if he wished he'd called in sick today and gone fishing. If I'd known how today was going to unfold, I would have considered going with him. "The medical examiner wants to talk to you before he takes the body."

"I'll be right there."

Greensmith hesitated as Hanlon hadn't broken her glare at Myra. I could see he was debating whether he should stay or not. With a small shrug of his shoulders he turned around and walked out. I almost asked him to take me with him.

"I don't want either of you leaving town. I will have more questions for you."

Myra rolled her eyes. "Where would I go? I've lived here my entire life." She paused as she glanced over at me. "On the other hand, Sadie has no ties to this town, nothing to keep her here…"

Good to see Myra was over the shock and back to her charming self. For a brief moment I had started to believe that even if we weren't friends, in this situation, we were at least allies. It seems I was wrong.

"I'll let you know if I need to go anywhere." I paused for a moment as I remembered something that would have been useful about half an hour earlier. "Also, if you need to speak to me, I would suggest you contact Tarquin Burroughs." I had a feeling my lawyer was not going to be happy about the predicament I had found myself in.

As she stood up, Hanlon threw a glare at both of us. "You can go for now, but if I find either one of you at another of my crime scenes, I will be arresting you on principle." She stalked away but stopped when she got to the door. "And, Miss Goodwin, you are not to speak about this with Sheriff Tolan."

I frowned. "I think I'm going to check with my advocate, but I'm pretty sure I can talk about my day with anyone I choose, and I would suggest trying to infringe on my civil rights is not the way to go here."

Hanlon froze, and I had a feeling that if she thought she could get away with it she would have torn me to pieces. Lucky for me, I had too many witnesses, at least for now.

I let the breath I had been holding out after she walked through the door and glanced over at Myra who had an indefinable look in her eyes.

"What?" I asked.

"I'm just trying to decide if you are incredibly brave or incredibly stupid."

I gave a small smile to the woman who I had just worked out liked me slightly more than the police officer who wanted to kill me painfully. "I'm leaning towards incredibly stupid."

Myra nodded sharply. "I think you're right."

21

*T*he ride back to my house was extremely quiet, and by quiet, I mean really uncomfortable. What do you say to a woman angered by your existence and who, in the space of a day, has broken into your house and you've discovered a body together? There is no small talk that can gloss over that kind of baggage. When we turned into my driveway, I stifled a groan. On top of a ladder using a hammer on the wall was the one person who could make this situation worse.

"Do you have any idea how many of us wanted that?" Myra said quietly.

"I'm perfectly aware of the sheriff's popularity in this town," I replied, not entirely sure where she was going with this.

"You don't understand. We may have all dated him, but none of us really had him."

Myra looked over at me with a small amount of sadness in her eyes and I felt bad for her. There was no denying Conall's appeal. I was still unsure how we had ended up in the place we were, but it seemed Destiny had decided I couldn't be trusted with finding my own happily ever after. Considering my romantic history, I was inclined to agree. It still didn't mean that I was completely comfortable with the situation I found myself in.

"Are you going to be okay?" I asked, keeping my eyes straight ahead.

"I'll be fine once you're out of my car."

And that meant the tender moment was over. I nodded sharply and got out of the vehicle. I didn't even look back as she pulled out of my driveway, my attention taken by the man climbing down the ladder.

"What are you doing?"

"What does it look like I'm doing?" he grumbled. "I'm working on your house. This place is a death trap."

"So I've been told. Repeatedly."

"Did you want to tell me why you got out of Myra Hallybread's car?" Conall asked when he reached the bottom of the ladder.

"I would suggest that you would be happier if you didn't know."

"I'm sure I would be, but I still think I'm going to need to know that information at some point. I generally find that it's better not to be blindsided."

"You're right," I sighed. "Come inside and I'll get you a drink."

When we were comfortably situated on the couch, I proceeded to explain to him how my day had unfolded. I could see the frown on his face growing deeper and deeper the further into the explanation I got.

"Let me see if I understand this," he said slowly. "Myra Hallybread broke into your house and instead of calling the sheriff, which most people would tell you is the next move you should make, you got into her car to visit her ex-boyfriend who is a suspect in the murder of his current girlfriend."

I nodded. That sounded about right.

"Do I need to tell you how many ways your actions today could have ended badly?"

Oh, that was precisely the wrong thing to say. "If you think that because you're my Destined Beloved you can get away with being condescending to me…"

Conall circled his finger in front of his face. "This is not the face of your freaking out Destined Beloved. This is the face of the sheriff in this town who is concerned about the actions of one of his citizens. Trust me when I say I would have said the same thing, with the same tone, to any of the people in this town who had done something as incredibly reckless as what you did today."

"Well, maybe if you adjusted that tone you might get a better outcome to your questioning," I muttered.

He stared at me and I knew that the reason I was feeling defensive was because he was absolutely right. All along I'd known that my actions today weren't smart, but sometimes my need to fix things outruns my common sense. I badly wanted Conall to have his job back and I wanted Brigitte Hanlon to be as far away from us as possible. I had a feeling that she was going to do her level best to destroy any chance of Conall and I having a future together. A future I was becoming more comfortable with in a surprisingly quick time frame.

"You're right." I could tell from the expression on Conall's face that I had managed to shock him. "I should have thought things through." I shook my head. "Everything is happening so fast and I don't understand any of it. Helping Myra today to find out what happened to her friend gave me a feeling of some control again."

I could see Conall struggling with what I said, and I felt a sudden surge of compassion. I was so caught up in dealing with what I was going through I kept forgetting that he had to put up with the same upheaval as I did, as well as dealing with the unfamiliar emotions of his newly discovered berserker side.

"I understand," he said slowly. "I just need you to think carefully before putting yourself in danger and, regardless of your reasoning, you put yourself in danger today for no real benefit."

Our conversation was interrupted by the front door opening. "Sadie, are you here?"

We looked up to find Tilda walking into the living room. She pulled up short at the sight of Conall and I sitting together.

"I should stop just walking into your house, shouldn't I?" she asked with a sheepish look on her face.

"That might be for the best," Conall said as he stood up. "I'd better go into work and see how much damage Detective Hanlon has done to my department."

"I'm hearing a lot of your staff are coming down with the flu," Tilda said helpfully.

"Great," muttered Conall. "Just what I needed." He dropped a kiss to my forehead. "Be safe."

Tilda and I watched him leave the house, and my friend looked back at me with stars in her eyes.

"It's so romantic."

I didn't have a response for her, so I decided to redirect the conversation. "How's your mother?"

Tilda snorted as she flopped down on the couch next to me. "My mother is a drama queen. My sister is way more sensible than my mother ever would be. She's not letting a werewolf get near her without a documented sexual history and a doctor's appointment."

I nodded. "Good to know."

"How's your new best friend?"

"I'm assuming you're talking about Myra."

"Word is she backed you up with Brigitte Hanlon."

I nodded.

"Didn't see that coming. I would have laid bets that those two would have turned off their hatred for each other long enough to completely roast you."

"Just goes to show that some things are eternal."

Tilda grinned. "So, did you want to explain to me exactly what happened. So far, all I've got are vague rumors and salacious innuendo. Entertaining as that has been, I'd rather know the truth."

For the second time that day, I explained what had happened since she left me alone with Myra.

"That was really stupid."

I had hoped for a little more support from Tilda.

"We were just going to ask Jaxon some questions," I said, defensively.

Tilda nodded. "I can see that. It would have been the reasonable thing to do if I was the one backing you up." She put up a hand to stop me as I tried to interrupt. "But you chose to go with Myra who, let's face it, would have tossed you in the path of an ax wielding maniac if he was still on scene."

No, she wouldn't," I protested, although there was a part of me that could see her doing exactly that.

"Really?" Tilda said. "From where I'm standing, she would have got rid of you from the sheriff's life and given herself time to escape. I'm not seeing a downside to those actions for her."

I could see her point. "Look, we don't need to go through this. Conall's already told me how idiotic my choices were today…"

"I'm not saying your choices were idiotic. I'm saying that

you should have waited for me to cover you. We would have still done the same things, you just would have had more reliable backup, and I would have probably got a warmer welcome from Jaxon."

"You knew him?" I asked.

"Course I knew him, we went to school together. He was an okay guy, a little clueless, but overall, he was pretty harmless. I was surprised to hear that he started going out with Jeanette. She's a little more high maintenance than I would have expected him to go for. Then again, he used to go out with Myra, so it looks like he had a type."

"Not for much longer," I mused. "He was pretty sure that Jeanette was cheating on him."

Tilda snapped her head up. "He told you that?" She shook her head. "That might explain... I can't believe she did that..."

I grabbed her arm as she stood up and looked like she was going to storm out of the house. "What's wrong? What did she do?"

Tilda stopped and seemed to collect herself. When she turned back to face me, she looked furious. "I know exactly what Jeanette has been doing, and I can't believe her nerve."

This did not look good, but as Tilda had said, we needed to have each other's back. "Where are we going?" I asked as I grabbed my bag for another trip.

She stopped as if to say something and then shrugged. "We're not doing anything too dangerous so I guess it will be safe enough for you to go."

I raised an eyebrow. "And when did we decide that you were going to start making decisions about where I could and could not go."

"When your soul got linked to our beloved berserker sheriff who could make my life severely unpleasant, if not end it in horrific fashion, if you got hurt in any way on my watch."

"So, your only concern is your own well-being, not mine?" I asked, not sure if I was going to be happy with her answer, no matter what it was.

"Absolutely."

I shrugged. "I'll do my best to never get hurt on your watch then."

"I would appreciate it."

22

"Where exactly are we going?" I looked out of the window and watched as we left the town and started heading for the forest. Normally I would have thought that we were heading for the coven library, but we had veered off the main road and were headed into an area that I was not familiar with.

"We need to talk to Henrietta."

I waited, and when Tilda didn't continue, I turned to look at her. "Let's imagine for a moment that I didn't grow up in this town, and that I have no idea who this Henrietta person is."

Tilda tilted her head to the side as if she was thinking very carefully. "Henrietta is a little difficult to explain." She paused as if deciding how to continue. "She's a banshee."

"A banshee," I repeated slowly. "You mean one of those female spirits who do the screaming when death is near."

Tilda nodded slowly. "Kind of."

"You're taking me to see a ghost?"

"Of course not. Banshees aren't ghosts. They are flesh and

blood women who have the ability to see death around those people they care about."

"But the screaming is real?"

"Oh yeah, the screaming is real. There's a reason most banshees live far away from populated areas. Nothing ruins a neighborhood like a banshee moving in.

"Is she able to talk?" I asked. "I thought banshees were only able to scream and wail."

Tilda grimaced. "That's where the situation gets complicated. Banshees are just like everyone else. They talk, they sing, they live their life as normal. They just have an uncontrollable urge to scream when they are around someone they know is going to die in a very short space of time. As you can imagine, that doesn't do much for their social lives. Most of them end up living as recluses, as far away from other people as they can possibly get."

"And that's why this Henrietta lives so far out here?"

"No, Henrietta lives out here for a completely different reason." Tilda took in a deep breath. "Henrietta went to school with my grandmother. Grandma said that she was very social, engaging and she loved life. She was dating a guy who adored her, and everyone was pretty sure they were going to get married straight after high school. She was pretty, popular, and on top of that she was truly kind. According to Grandma there was nobody who could say a bad word about her."

I waited as Tilda paused in the story as if she was struggling.

"One day, Henrietta and her boyfriend were hanging out together after school with a group of their friends when all of a sudden she looks up at her boyfriend and starts wailing as if her heart was breaking. Everyone knew that the only reason for the banshee wail would be because her boyfriend was going to die."

"I'm assuming he didn't react well," I said, quietly.

Tilda shook her head and I could see that her eyes were glassy with unshed tears.

"We all know that a banshee's wail means death and there is no way to get away from that. She couldn't stop wailing. Their friends started freaking out and he just panicked. He ran away from her, got in his car and sped out of the parking lot. An hour later that car was found wrapped around a tree. Henrietta's boyfriend didn't survive the crash."

I could feel the tears building behind my eyes. "That's a terrible story."

"The worst part was Henrietta blamed herself. She thought that she caused the crash. If only she hadn't screamed around him, he might not have crashed his car."

"That poor girl," I murmured. "That must have been devastating. No wonder she hides out here."

"She went further than just hiding. Henrietta went to a witch who swore she could take the banshee wail away from her."

I frowned. "Is that possible?"

Tilda shrugged. "I don't know if it would be possible, but Henrietta was desperate to try. At that stage it's safe to say that there was a great deal of grief and self-loathing involved."

"What happened?" Even though I asked the question, I wasn't sure if I wanted the answer. The expression on Tilda's face told me there would not be a happy ending to this story.

Tilda swallowed as if something was stuck in her throat. "The spell removed Henrietta's wail. It also took away her ability to talk, see and hear."

"That's terrible."

"Yeah," Tilda said quietly. "She came back to Walker Bay and found the most isolated place in the county to move into. Grandma used to take me to visit her all the time when I was a kid. Sometimes I'll drop off herbs that she needs and have a little chat." Tilda gave a small smile. "She's been very interested in Flora having a new niece all of a sudden. I'm pretty sure she went to school with your grandmother."

I was suddenly struck by a thought. "What happened to the witch who did the spell?"

Tilda shrugged. "I don't know. I would have thought that a crime like that would have drawn a swift response from the Conclave, but I've never heard that part of the story."

Any more questions I had would have to wait as we pulled up at a small house in the deepest part of the forest. Tilda pulled out her phone and started to text.

"What are you doing?" I asked.

Tilda smiled. "It's a courtesy thing I do. She always has her phone on vibrate in her pocket." She waved her phone in the air. "I send her a message, so she knows by the vibrations that somebody is coming in. That way she isn't taken by surprise when we walk into her house and put a hand on her shoulder."

"Sounds like you guys have worked out a good system," I said.

"When I came as a kid, everyone learned to use this language with her where we did signs on the palm of her hand. It took ages to learn, but at least we could communicate. There's a few of us who come to visit to make sure she doesn't get too lonely."

I put my hand on her arm. "You know, you're a really good person."

Tilda ducked her head and smiled shyly. "I just don't think anybody should be alone."

"A lot of people think that, but you do something about it. That's what makes a good person."

As we walked up to the door, I took note of the immaculate garden and smiled inwardly. I had no doubt that if she truly wanted to, Henrietta had the gardening talent to grow her own herbs despite her disabilities. The fact she didn't showed that she enjoyed Tilda's visits.

If somebody had asked me what I thought the house of a person who had been robbed of their senses was like, I would have said dark. Henrietta's house was full of light, all of the windows were wide open and sunlight came streaming into every room.

"She likes to feel the heat of the sun and the breeze on her skin," Tilda supplied.

I could understand that. From what Tilda said, touch was one of the only senses that the banshee had left. When we found Henrietta, she was in a room with large windows, her face pointing towards the sunlight. Tilda started stomping on the floor as she walked over, and it took a moment for me to realize that she was providing a slight vibration in the floorboards to give Henrietta warning that she was approaching. Henrietta stuck out her hand and Tilda grasped it. I watched in fascination as Tilda's hand moved in Henrietta's palm, and then their hands switched position as she answered. I found a chair and sat down while watching this conversation taking place in complete silence. Ten minutes later the conversation stopped, and Tilda waved me over.

"She wants to meet you."

I stepped up to the two of them and put my hand out hesitantly. Tilda guided it to Henrietta's and the slight woman clasped it with a strength that surprised me. She gave it a tug and I leaned forward. Her other hand slid up my arm, over my shoulder and neck and rested on my face.

"Don't panic," murmured Tilda. "She just wants to get an idea of what you look like."

I stood patiently as Henrietta slowly explored every part of my face. After what seemed an interminable amount of time she stopped and stuck her hand in the air. Tilda grabbed hold and they restarted their conversation. No longer wanted, I retreated back to my chair and sat in the silent room, my eyes intent on the compelling scene in front of me. Half an hour later Tilda gave Henrietta a quick hug, but I noted the tension around her eyes. At some point in that conversation, Tilda had discovered something she was not happy with. Feeling that it would be disrespectful to start asking questions in front of Henrietta, even though she couldn't hear them, I waited until we were outside.

"What did she tell you?" I asked.

"She said she's felt a witch around the property, but she didn't know who it was."

I couldn't help the skeptical frown. "She felt a witch?"

Tilda nodded as her eyes scanned the forest surrounding the house. "It seems to be a by-product of the spell that took her senses. She can feel magic users and can differentiate between those she's familiar with and those she doesn't know. For the last couple of months she's been getting a whiff of a magic user being around, but it was never anything definitive. When there weren't any obvious problems, she dismissed it as being unimportant."

"But you think differently."

"Yes," she opened the car door and started to get in.

"Where are we going?" I asked as I joined her.

"Two weeks ago, when I came to visit Henrietta, I saw Jeanette's car on the road heading to town."

"Could she have been visiting someone else out here?" I fastened my seatbelt as Tilda started us down what would generously be called a track.

"Not likely, and I have a bit of a hunch where she was coming from." Her hands tightened on the wheel as the car lurched to one side after hitting a particularly deep pothole.

I looked around doubtfully. "I don't know Jeanette as well

as you do, but she didn't really strike me as the kind of woman who enjoyed roughing it."

Tilda barked out a shot of laughter. "You would be right under normal circumstances, but I have a feeling these circumstances were far from normal."

We lapsed into silence until we pulled up into a small clearing with a tiny cottage in the middle of it.

"What is this?" I asked as we got out of the car.

"Henrietta lets me wander the property because some plants that I sell are more potent when they're grown in the wild than when I grow them. I found this cottage during one of those walks. I'd never heard about it before, so I assumed nobody knew it existed." She smiled ruefully. "If anyone had known about it when we were in high school, it would have become a major party house. None of us would have been able to resist a place this perfect."

"It looks pristine," I mused. "It can't have been here very long.

Tilda laughed. "It's a spell a lot of witches with property use. It keeps the place in the condition of the day of the spell, and prevents them from having to come back and clean it all the time."

It's funny, I'd always thought of magic being used for mystical reasons like a quest for lost treasure or an adventure. Here in Walker Bay, I was discovering it was more often used for mundane reasons to make life easier, in the same way normal people used technology.

As we walked towards the cottage, I started feeling a bit queasy and my heart sank as I realized that I'd had that feeling before. A closer look confirmed my suspicions and I grabbed hold of Tilda's arm to prevent her taking a step closer.

"We need to call Flora."

23

I could tell by the time that Flora arrived that Tilda was not happy with me. She seemed even less happy when Flora took her to one side and, after an animated conversation, Tilda left with barely a glance in my direction.

I waited until Tilda's car was out of sight. "I think we have a…"

"Not just yet," Flora interrupted.

I waited impatiently. This place was giving me the creeps and I knew night was going to be falling soon. It had been a long day already. The last thing I wanted was to be stuck here after dark.

"Okay, we should be safe now," she said before turning to me. "Can I assume that the reason you called me so urgently is because we have another little problem?"

I eyed the now familiar writhing mass of black tendrils that encircled the cottage. "I would call this one a big problem," I pointed to about a foot from the base of the building. "From what I can see the curse surrounds the entire cottage.

I'm assuming that it would go off on someone if they step too close to the cottage, like a booby trap."

Flora rubbed her forehead. "Well, that's just charming. Do we have any idea who could have set it?"

"The current theory is that Jeanette was out here recently." I shrugged. "Whether she was the one who set it, or it was someone else is anybody's guess."

"Great, just great," Flora muttered. She looked at me expectantly. "Do you think you can deal with it?"

"I guess," I hedged. "I'm hoping the tablet is around here somewhere." I looked down at the writhing mass at my feet. "Knowing my luck, it's buried under some of these." I dropped to my knees and started going to work.

"I think Tilda is suspicious," I said quietly.

"Of course, she's suspicious," snapped Flora. "That doesn't mean she is going to make the leap to you being a curse-breaker."

"We hope," I mumbled. "I feel bad keeping things from her. She has been nothing but good to me since the moment she found me in the trunk of her grandmother's car."

Flora grabbed my shoulders and pulled me up. "You cannot tell her. The more people who know about you, the more chance of you being discovered by the Conclave. I won't let that happen." The fear in her eyes was real and haunting.

"I won't tell her, but we have to be prepared if she finds out. Tilda's smart and observant. If anyone is going to work out what I am, it's going to be her."

"Then we will deal with that situation if it happens," Flora said, resolutely. "Until that time comes, I want you to be very careful. We don't know when the magister is going to arrive and, until the investigation is over, we need to protect the knowledge about what you are at all times."

"I will, I promise." I turned back to the tendrils and

started picking at them again. It was interesting, in a morbid way, to watch them go from looking like a pile of squirming snakes to falling apart when I touched them. It was also pretty disgusting. I was going to stock up on a boat load of hand sanitizer if this was going to be a regular occurrence.

"Have you had any indication what the curse would have done if someone had crossed the threshold?"

I was surprised by Flora's question. "No, is that something I'm supposed to know?"

She watched me quizzically as I'd pick at tendrils she couldn't see, and then shake them to the ground as they disintegrated, with what I'm sure was an appalled expression on my face.

"I've been trying to find out as much as I can, and I came across a piece of writing which indicated you should be able to tell who created the curse, how they created it, and what its effect is supposed to be."

I looked down at the dying tendrils in my hands. "All I'm getting at the moment is a slightly queasy feeling in my stomach."

"You could try concentrating," she said gently. "Maybe there's a way to communicate with the curse. Some of my reading indicates the reason curses are so strong is because they become almost a living entity."

I grimaced at that observation. I was pretty sure that starting to believe these things were alive was going to make this ability of mine so much worse.

I held up one of the tendrils and looked at it, concentrating as hard as I could. My mind stayed blank. Actually, that wasn't exactly true. I was horrified when I started thinking how hungry I was.

"I'm not getting anything," I announced, choosing to ignore the image of a cheeseburger that was flying through my brain.

"Maybe it will come to you," she remarked in a manner that was far more optimistic than I felt.

For the next hour I painstakingly pulled apart the curse. I could feel fatigue setting in and I wondered when I would find the tablet that controlled this mess.

"How's it going?" asked Flora, her voice deceptively calm. I could tell that she wasn't coping well with the fact that I was the one doing all the heavy lifting in this situation.

I turned and sighed. "Frustrating. I'm pretty sure that these things are a part of the curse, but also that they protect and hide the tablet that is used to create the curse. I just wish I knew a way to shortcut this part of the process."

The expression on Flora's face was speculative. "Have you thought that maybe by doing what you're doing now you are weakening the curse enough that you are able to destroy the tablet?"

"I guess that's a possibility," I mused. "It would explain why they exist. If the tendrils are the physical manifestation of the curse, the more I destroy, the weaker the curse becomes. Once I destroy enough of them the curse is weakened to the point that I am able to break it by smashing the tablet."

Flora looked thoughtful. "It's a solid hypothesis. We just need to test it."

I grunted. "I'm all for science, but I'm really hoping we don't get enough of these curses to test the theory properly… Wait a minute."

"What is it?" Flora asked with a worried expression.

"I think I found the mother lode. There's a clump of these things, and they look to be curling around something rather than just aimless wriggling like the rest of them."

Finding this clump tightly woven together, I decided that rather than pulling them apart one by one, I would just thrust my hands into the middle of it. And yes, it was just as disgusting as it sounded. There was some resistance, but gradually the tendrils disintegrated like all the others.

"Is it there?"

I looked down at the bare ground. "Do you by any chance have a shovel in your car?"

Flora groaned. "She buried it."

I wiped my hand across my forehead and grimaced when I noticed a small piece of a tendril was still attached to it. "I think so. I find it hard to believe those things were protecting a patch of dirt, so I think we need to dig." Or rather, I needed to dig. I wasn't going to risk letting Flora anywhere near this curse, not after her last experience. At least in this situation I was able to protect her.

Flora came back with a small gardening spade and passed it to me. "This is the best I can do."

I shrugged and went to work digging at the ground. It wasn't long before I heard the tell-tale sound of metal hitting stone. "I think I've found it," I said as I cleared the dirt away. Sure enough, there was the kind of stone I was reluctantly becoming familiar with. I pulled it out of the dirt and raised it high above my head, preparing to smash it against the ground when Flora called out.

"Stop!"

I lowered my arm. "Why would you possibly not want me to do this?"

"We could learn from it," she replied.

I shook my head. "No way, I know you can't see the things that I can see around this hunk of rock, but believe me, it is bad juju. There is no way that I want to learn how to do these things."

Flora smiled gently. "You have no idea how glad I am to hear that. I don't want you to learn how to create a curse either. I was hoping if you focus on the tablet, you'd be able to get some idea who did this and why they did it."

I contemplated that for a moment. "I guess it couldn't hurt."

I held the tablet in front of me and emptied my mind. Part of me was worried that it wouldn't work, and part was worried that it would work. Just as I was about to give up, I felt a sharp pain streak through my skull. Images slammed into me like a freight train. My brain had trouble keeping up, and I felt my body tense under the onslaught. I faintly heard Flora calling to me, but it was like I was no longer in control. I was sure I was burning with fever until a cool hand landed on my arm. A part of me knew it was Flora and I wanted to tell her to stay back, that it was too dangerous for her. Pain lanced through me and I could feel the power of the curse like a siren's song, trying to seduce me into embracing it. With what little strength I seemed to have left, I flung the tablet as far away from me as I could. My mind cleared, blackness rolled through and I crumpled to the ground.

24

I lurched upwards suddenly gripping my head. "Son of a... I am never doing that again." I opened my eyes and squinted in the harshness of the light, barely making out the shape of my aunt.

She knelt down next to me. "Is there anything I can do to help?"

I took stock of the way I was feeling. "You could hit me on the head with the garden spade and knock me out again. I'm pretty sure that's the only thing that is going to make me feel better."

"Let's try standing you up," Flora suggested, completely ignoring my wishes.

I groaned as she pulled me to my feet. "What happened?"

Flora kept her hands on my arms as I swayed while trying desperately to stay upright.

"Well, you were holding the tablet and then your body went incredibly stiff like you were having a seizure. You screamed and threw the tablet away.

"I don't remember screaming."

"But you remember the rest?" Flora kept stroking her

hand up and down my arm as if she couldn't believe I was still here.

"I'm pretty sure that I'm going to be reliving those moments in my nightmares for years to come." I frowned as I swiped at my face. "Did I fall in a puddle? It feels like I've got mud on my face."

Flora caught my hands and showed me the palms which were wet with blood. "You were gripping the tablet so tight the jagged edges cut into your hands. Some of it's on your face from when you grabbed your head."

I watched the blood oozing from between my fingers when a horrible thought struck me. "My blood mixing with the tablet isn't going to cause something awful to happen, is it?"

"No, you're immune to curses. You should be okay."

Despite her reassurance I couldn't help thinking that bleeding on a tablet of evil was not something I should repeat.

"Come with me." Flora pulled insistently on my upper arm and I followed her to the car.

She sat me down gently and reached in to get a first aid kit. As if she was dealing with a child, she cleaned off the blood and bandaged my wounds. It had been a while since I'd had somebody taking care of me. I had to admit that a part of me enjoyed it. She wet a piece of cloth and started dabbing at my head. When she'd finished, she leaned back and looked at me critically.

"That's the best I can do. It's not great, but you no longer look like you've been attacked."

That was comforting. Something niggled at the back of my mind. "The tablet, what happened to it?" I gasped. I could not believe that I'd forgotten about it.

"Over there," Flora indicated with her head. "You

slammed it down on the ground so hard it disintegrated on contact. All that's left of it is dust and rubble."

"Good," I said, roughly. After what I had just experienced, I knew without a doubt that thing needed to be destroyed. I just hoped that the knowledge of how to create it had died with Jeanette.

"What did you see?" Flora asked, her hand stroking my arm as if to provide me with some comfort.

I forced myself to pull back the images that had been blasted at me and concentrate on them. "Jeanette cast the curse. She was definitely having an affair with somebody and she knew that she couldn't take a chance on anyone finding out about it." My mouth went dry. "The curse was designed to cause hallucinations in whoever crossed the line she set up around the building. The victim wouldn't know whether what they were seeing was real or imagined. It wouldn't take long for the curse to send them insane. There was no particular victim in mind. It could have happened to anyone." I looked up helplessly. "This curse was beyond evil. It could have been a child that wandered over to the cottage. Tilda almost stepped right into it. It's one thing to target somebody with a curse, but this one could have taken out any number of innocents. Why would she have done something like that?"

Flora stared grimly at the cottage. "There must be something inside there worth her soul, because that's what she would have had to sacrifice to perform that kind of dark magic."

I pulled myself up. "Then let's find out what it is and expose it."

I didn't bother being careful as I stomped up to the front door of the cottage. What Jeanette had unleashed on this land was reckless and dangerous. It showed a selfishness that was breathtaking. All to cover up an affair. To say that I was angry was an understatement. Considering the effort Jeanette had taken to protect this place, I was surprised to find the front door was unlocked. Of course, normal security precautions weren't necessary when a curse of apocalyptic proportions was surrounding the building. I pushed the door open and walked inside, Flora following closely behind.

"Well, this is a little underwhelming." I don't know what I had been expecting but a one room cottage with a bed dominating the main area was not it.

"Considering this entire situation was about hiding an affair, this room contains everything they need," Flora remarked dryly.

"They could have at least made the bed after they were finished." I couldn't help the disgust I was feeling. I would normally say that using curses was wrong for any reason, but to use something that could cause so much damage just to hide an affair. My mind was having trouble understanding how anyone could be so utterly uncaring of other people. "We need to find who she was having the affair with. They're the most likely suspect in her murder."

"Wait," Flora stopped me as I started to walk to the other side of the room. "We're not here to work out who killed her."

I stopped, a confused look on my face. "Why not? I thought that was the entire reason we were here."

Flora gripped her hands tightly together. "What I mean is that finding Jeanette's killer is not our first priority. It's law enforcement's job to find who killed her. Our job is to find if there is anything in this cottage related to that curse and make sure it doesn't fall into anybody else's hands. After we've looked, I'll call Detective Hanlon and let her know that we've found a scene that could possibly be related to Jeanette's murder."

I looked down at my hands and noted that blood was seeping through the bandages.

"Sadie," Flora said gently. "I know you want to find out who did this, and I promise you that if we discover anything that is relevant I will make sure Hanlon gets it, but our first priority has to be ensuring that curse never sees the light of day again." Her eyes beseeched me to understand.

I nodded abruptly and took a deep breath. "Okay, what am I looking for?

Flora smiled and patted my arm. "We're looking for anything that's written down or items that may have been used in the creation of the curse. Books, papers, a knife to cut the skin to bind blood to the curse, some curses have been written on leather made of human skin."

"What kind of demented person would use human skin to write a curse?" I was horrified.

"The kind of person that would create a curse that sends people insane," Flora shot back.

"Point taken." I turned to start the hunt. "Make sure you don't touch anything," I said, helpfully. "We don't want to leave any evidence for Detective Hanlon."

Flora rolled her eyes. "I watch crime shows too. Anyway, it's too late. Your prints are already on the front doorknob. Probably some blood too. It's not like we're going to try to hide that we were here. We're just going to tell Detective Hanlon the truth."

"Except for the part about the monster curse surrounding this place," I remarked dryly.

"Except for that part. By the way, you're clumsy and fell over. That's how you hurt your hands."

I smiled at my aunt. "I'm sure that won't be much of a stretch for her to believe. She already doesn't have the best opinion of me."

"She thinks you took the one thing in this world that she badly wanted. She will never accept that."

"I didn't take Conall. He's a person, not a coffee machine. I never asked to be part of a Destined Beloved prophecy," I couldn't help the defensive tone in my voice.

Flora's tone softened. "I know you didn't, and I know you have been thrown into a situation you have no control over. You need to be very careful when dealing with Brigitte Hanlon. The kind of obsession that she has always had for Sheriff Tolan does not die easily. I suggest you never turn your back on her."

"I wasn't planning to," I muttered. I pressed my hand to my stomach as a wave of nausea hit me. "There's something here and it's close." I stepped towards the kitchen area and the nausea started to fade away. I started making my way around the cottage playing the worst hot and cold game ever. I finally realized the inescapable truth.

"I feel the most sick when I'm near the bed."

"That's not surprising," muttered Flora.

As I got nearer to the source of my nausea, a feeling of dread hit me and it felt familiar. There was nothing obvious that I could see on the bed, and I was reluctant to go searching through the mussed sheets, so I went to look under the bed. "Found something." I pulled a small wooden box out from where it was hiding. The nausea was strong, and my hands were shaking as I opened it up. Inside was a single page with writing and images on it.

"Is that it?" Flora asked, keeping her distance.

"I would say so." I squinted at the writing and as I did images started forming in my mind. I saw myself as assured and powerful, able to command whole armies and have anybody I wanted doing my bidding. I heard a soft seductive voice in my ear telling me all I could accomplish if I would only take the curse on as my own. I slammed the box shut. "We need to burn this, we need to do it now."

Flora was instantly alert. "Shouldn't we study it, see if there's anything more to it."

I scrambled to my feet. "That is the last thing we should do. Now, I need you to tell me the best way to destroy this thing. If we can't do it using magic, we need to find some lighter fluid and a box of matches, or a missile strike. I really don't care which way we go, but we need to eliminate it now."

Understanding that I was not in any mood to negotiate, Flora went through the cupboards and found what we were looking for.

"We need to go outside to do this unless you want to explain to Hanlon what we were doing setting things on fire in here." She held the lighter fluid and matches out in front of her.

Personally, considering the dark magic that was done here, I would be more than happy to watch the place burn. Unfortunately, I could see how that wasn't an option. "We can't do it anywhere near here. Do you know of someplace that is secluded and where there is no chance of us being seen? I have a feeling this thing is not going to go quietly."

I put the box in the trunk of the car, wanting it as far away from me as possible. Doing that muted the voices, but I could still hear them and their alluring messages.

"How long until we get there?" I said through gritted teeth.

"Not long." Flora took a hand off the wheel and gripped my own. "I don't know what's going on, but you're stronger than this."

I really hoped I was because this wasn't like anything I'd faced before.

The car braked suddenly. "We need to walk the rest of the way," Flora said, regretfully.

Well, that was just great. The last thing I needed right now was more exercise.

I grabbed the box while Flora gathered the lighting fluid and matches, and we headed deeper into the forest. Fortunately, we only needed to walk a few minutes before we reached a clearing.

Flora spread her arms out. "This is a protected circle. There are wards embedded into this area to prevent anyone spying on it, and nobody can hear what happens in here."

That sounded great. I dropped the box to the ground, grabbed the lighter fluid and covered it liberally. I struck the match and dropped it. Luckily, Flora pulled me back, because there was instantly a whoosh and flames shot up. If I'd stayed in my original position, I would have gone up with it.

"Are you out of your mind?" Flora hissed.

I could see her mouth working but my mind couldn't catch what she was saying. There was screaming in my head. Screams of pain. Screams of retribution. I dropped to my knees and started sobbing. I stayed like that for what felt like hours but was more likely only a few minutes. Finally, the screaming stopped and there was blessed peace in my head. I opened my eyes and found that Flora had sat on the ground next to me. I had curled up on my side with my head in her lap, her hand stroking my hair, crooning to me as if I was a child.

I sniffed loudly as I tried wiping away the tears that stubbornly refused to stop streaming down my face. "This is a little humiliating."

Flora laughed quietly. "There's no need to be embarrassed. What you just did required a lot of strength."

I wasn't going to argue with her. I struggled to sit up and

watched the flames dancing against the rising shadows. "Did you hear anything?"

"No," Flora said quietly. "What did you hear?"

"I think Jeanette was trying to control someone. That curse was designed to enslave a person. Like a love spell, but so much worse. It wanted me to keep it, to use it. It was like a living thing trying to seduce me with images of power. They were really hard to say no to." I swallowed nervously. "Then after I set it on fire it tried to hurt me, and it threatened me. I don't know what that was, but it was more than a normal curse." I turned around to Flora, hoping desperately that she would have the answer. "The last time I broke a curse didn't hurt nearly as much as this time. I thought the tablet was bad, but that piece of paper was like a living thing and it was beyond evil. How am I supposed to deal with things like that squirming through my head?" I started feeling hysterical again. If this was what being a cursebreaker meant, then I wanted no part of it.

Flora put her arms around me. "You're stronger than you think," she murmured. "To be a cursebreaker you have to be."

We sat there in silence for a long time, watching the flames die down as the evening turned to night.

When the fire had put itself out, Flora turned to me and pushed my hair away from my face. "Let's go home."

I groaned as I stood up and walked over to the pile of ashes. With my foot I spread the ashes around as if trying to break up any chance of them coming back together. After the day I just had, I no longer cared if I was acting rationally or not.

"Don't we need to stay here and talk to Hanlon about the cottage?" I asked, my voice sounding sluggish to my own ears.

Flora put her hand on my arm and started leading me back to the car. "No, I'm taking you home and then I'll contact her. If she has any questions for you, I'll tell her to speak to you in the morning."

I snorted indelicately. "You really think she's going to listen to you."

"She may not want to, but she will have no choice but to accede to the wishes of the coven leader when it comes to the well-being of one of my witches." Flora's expression was grim, and I had no doubt that, at least for tonight, I was safe.

Back at my house I sat quietly as Flora re-bandaged my hands.

"I didn't do you any favors with this place, did I?" she said ruefully.

"I love it." I could tell I'd surprised her. "There's something about it. It feels like it could be a home." I didn't know any other way to explain how I felt about this house. It was like I belonged. "Once I get a day to myself, I'm going to hunt down the curse and get rid of it. After that I'm going to do some work on it and get some new furniture. Just wait and see. Once I've finished, you're not going to recognize this place."

"I like that," Flora said quietly. "This place could use a new start."

I watched her as she continued working and noticed the frown that seemed to have taken permanent residence on her face since we'd found the curse.

"What's the problem, other than the fact we just had to destroy another curse and my brain almost got blasted out of my head?"

Flora looked as if she was trying to give me a gentle smile, but it wasn't quite working in the way she thought it was. "I've been thinking about Jeanette and that curse." She sighed heavily. "Creating a curse is not something that just anyone can do. When we discovered that Isobel created the curse that trapped me, I was surprised that she betrayed me like that, but I wasn't surprised that she was capable of doing it. She was my friend, but she was smart and ambitious. She was also the librarian, so that gave her access to information that other people would not have had. The curse on your house was the product of an old family book which hadn't been turned in. The witch who cast that curse may have been a little unhinged but, at her best, she had some serious power." Flora finished the bandaging and patted my arm. "Jeanette was not one of the sharpest tools in the shed. She was one of those women who got ahead through the men she was with. I don't see her having the intelligence or ambition to do this."

I contemplated what she said. "That doesn't change what I saw. Jeanette was the one who placed that curse around that building. She did it to ensure that not only was the cottage protected, but if anyone got too close, they would be sent insane. Despite what you may think of Jeanette, that curse was vicious. There must be something we're missing here."

25

I wish I could say that I didn't dream that night. I'd hoped that I was so exhausted that my mind would just shut down, but the day had been too intense for me to get away with a peaceful sleep. Despite my belief that I would only have nightmares, all I'd heard throughout the night was that low seductive voice trying to convince me to take the power that only I could wield. I woke up afraid and confused. I was now more convinced than ever that I had not seen the last of that evil. I only hoped I was strong enough to withstand it.

I caught sight of myself in the mirror as I got up and shuddered. My restless night had wreaked havoc on my hair. I wasn't going to worry about it until I'd had my shower. What I needed was a drink of water. I headed downstairs only to be brought up short by the sight that greeted me. There, in my living room, was my half-dressed Destined Beloved.

"What are you doing on my couch?" I asked as I swiped the hair from my eyes and tried to ensure I wasn't staring at his bare chest. I don't think I was as successful as I hoped I would be when he smirked at me.

Conall sat up, the blanket dropping to his waist, providing me with an even better view. "I'm protecting you, what does it look like I'm doing?"

"It looks like you came into my house without my permission and made yourself at home. I'm pretty sure any law enforcement officer worth his salt would call that breaking and entering. I'm positive I locked my front door last night."

Conall grabbed a shirt and pulled it over his head, thus depriving me of the best morning view I'd had in a long time. "You did. Well done on that, by the way. Most witches believe that their wards are enough to protect them and don't bother with locking their doors."

I wondered what happened to the wards Flora had put in place. If they were still working, I should have woken up to a sheriff sized crystal ornament. That would have made an interesting phone call to my aunt.

As if he knew what I was thinking, Conall grinned. "Flora gave me a spare key and told me she had placed an exemption in the wards for me."

"Really?" I knew I looked perplexed. That didn't sound like something a protective aunt would do.

He leaned back on the couch and gave me a flirtatious grin. "She figured we'd need it sooner or later. I'm kind of hoping for sooner."

That was simply not fair. Up until now, Conall had been mostly serious with me. That side of him I could handle. Barely. I don't think I had a defense against this relaxed and flirty version of the sheriff. I could see myself getting used to it very quickly. Not to mention the way he seemed to fit into my new home.

"Flora called me last night to tell me about Jeanette being

seen out at a cottage on Henrietta's property. She said you went out there with Tilda and found evidence of her having an affair."

"When Myra raised Jaxon's spirit after we found his body, he told us he suspected she was cheating on him. Tilda remembered seeing her out near Henrietta's property. We just followed the breadcrumbs."

Conall ran his hand through his hair. "I need you to realize that following the breadcrumbs can be dangerous." He looked meaningfully at my bandaged hands. "You already got hurt. I don't like that." He cleared his throat. "Even though Flora contacted me I had to tell Hanlon so she could be the one gathering evidence."

I was a bit surprised by that. "Do you trust her?"

Conall grimaced. "Not as far as I can throw her. That's why, before I contacted her, I went out there last night with Deputy Iverson and got my own samples. They've already been sent off to a private lab, separate to what Hanlon is doing."

I hated to think what kind of samples the two men had to collect. "That must have been unpleasant."

Conall smiled. "Not exactly the best part of the job, but if it solves the case it's worth it."

He sobered as his eyes travelled the length of my body. "How are you feeling? I know you were pretty restless when I checked on you."

"You came into my bedroom while I was asleep?"

He nodded. "I was worried about you."

"That doesn't make that statement any less creepy."

Conall's eyes sparkled. "So, if I said I stood there watching you sleeping…"

"I'd be calling the cops."

He laughed. "I didn't, though I may in future. I just intend to be a lot closer than your bedroom door when I do it."

I rolled my eyes at the assumption. "I never took you for an optimist."

He dropped his voice and growled. "It's going to happen."

I was realistic enough not to deny the statement. "I'm going to get something to eat. Do you want anything?"

"I checked your pantry. You don't seem to have a huge amount of options. How about breakfast at the diner?"

I stopped heading for the kitchen. "With you?"

Conall stood up and I was both grateful and disappointed to see he was wearing sweats under that blanket. "Of course, with me. I figured it's about time we stopped dancing around this prophecy and made a decent attempt to get to know each other."

I couldn't see a problem with that thinking. "Okay, I'll have a shower first and then you can have yours."

Conall gave me a slow grin. "Or we could have the shower together and save water."

I grinned back at him. "Or I could kick you out now for trying to leapfrog over the getting to know you stage."

Conall shrugged. "Message received. Just fair warning, I'm not the kind to give up easily." He paused. "Or take things slowly."

"Well, there's a shocking piece of news," I said as I headed back upstairs.

After my shower I took a bit more care with my clothes than I would have normally. I was pretty sure that a first date with your Destined Beloved was supposed to be a special occasion. My usual habit of choosing comfort over style was not going to quite make it today.

I went downstairs and found Conall in the kitchen looking through messages on his phone. "Shower's free."

Conall looked up and if I had any doubt about what I was wearing, the heat in his eyes calmed my nerves. "You look amazing."

I could have said something witty in that moment, but I was captured in his gaze. "Thank you," I whispered.

He strode toward me and pulled me close. "I just want one kiss, just one," he growled.

I barely had time to nod before he dropped his head and crushed his mouth on mine. My hands travelled up his arms, feeling the corded strength in them, and entwined behind his neck. He tilted my head and took the kiss deeper. Even though he kept his hands still on my hips it felt like he was touching me everywhere. I couldn't help the moan that came from deep within me. I had never felt this way before and all he'd done was kiss me. I wanted it to go on forever, but he abruptly pulled back. The two of us stared at each other, breathing heavily.

Conall swallowed thickly. "I'll have my shower."

I almost groaned thinking of him being wet and naked in my house. "Good idea. I'll…I'll wait for you here."

He watched me for a few more seconds then backed away and headed upstairs to the bathroom. Once he was out of sight I dropped to the couch and put my head between my knees, hoping that would stop it from spinning. I wondered if this kind of attraction was part of the prophecy or whether it would have happened anyway. It didn't matter. I had a feeling that my future was now set. I needed something to distract me or I was going to jump him the second he got out of that shower. As if in answer to my plea to the universe I heard a knock on the front door. I pulled myself up, grateful that the dizziness seemed to have faded, and internally groaned as I opened the door and found the universe had a sick sense of humor.

"How can I help you, Detective Hanlon?"

She gave me and my outfit a quick once over and gave me a look that indicated that she found me lacking. I would have felt self-conscious if it hadn't been for Conall's earlier response to the exact same outfit.

"I believe I need to speak to you, Ms Goodwin, about your interference in a crime scene yesterday."

I frowned. "Unless sex in this town is against the law, I don't know how it would be a crime scene."

"No, but trespassing is illegal, and Jeanette Hocking did not have permission to be on that land."

There was no response to the serious way she made that statement. "Come in." I opened the door wide and waved her into my house. Yet again she sniffed as she looked around. Looked like nothing about me impressed her. I could live with that.

I heard the bathroom door slam shut and Conall charged down the stairs, still buttoning up his uniform shirt.

"What are you doing here?" he barked.

"My job," Hanlon shot back, clearly disturbed to find the sheriff in my house. "What are you doing here?"

Conall stopped next to me and wrapped an arm around my waist. "I wouldn't think it would be unusual for me to spend the night with my Destined Beloved."

I was faced with two opposing feelings. On one hand, I couldn't help melting a little bit when he claimed me as his Destined Beloved in front of other people. On the other, every time he did it in front of Detective Hanlon, she got this look on her face and I was a bit afraid she was going to have a stroke.

"Detective Hanlon is here to talk to me about the cottage."

The look on Conall's face was comical. "What's there to talk about? She just found it. It wasn't like she'd been there before."

"I just wanted to clarify some details," Detective Hanlon said, her irritation at his questioning on full display.

Conall looked at me.

"I had never been out there before. I didn't even know the place existed before we visited Henrietta yesterday."

"With Tilda, right?" Hanlon asked.

"Yes, with Tilda. She remembered seeing Jeanette out on that road and thought it was strange. We thought we'd check it out."

By this time, Hanlon was writing furiously in a notebook. "When you got to the cottage you called your aunt. Is that correct?"

"Yes."

"Why exactly did you do that? I mean, you just found the cottage. Henrietta gave you permission to search it. I wouldn't have imagined you would be able to stop yourself from having a look."

Fortunately, Flora and I had gone over the story to tell Hanlon the night before, or else I would have gone to pieces right about this point. "With everything else going on Flora told me to call her before doing anything stupid. I figured walking into an unknown cottage where a murder victim may have spent her last days qualified."

"Is that why you sent Tilda away?" Hanlon asked.

This was where it got tricky. On the surface there was no good reason to not allow Tilda to enter the cottage. The fact she would have learned my big secret if she remained was not something I was willing to share with the woman who would happily deliver me to the Conclave on a silver platter.

"Flora felt that the less people there would minimize the contamination if there was any evidence that needed to be collected."

"Yet she let you in."

I nodded. "I had been with Myra when we spoke to Jaxon's spirit. She thought that would be helpful."

"Did she?" Hanlon mused. "And did you possibly find anything or remove anything from the scene?"

I frowned at her insinuation. "Are you asking if we stole something? Why would we do that?"

Hanlon shrugged. "I'm not entirely sure why you do anything. I still don't have a satisfactory answer how you hurt yourself."

I held up my bandaged hands. "I tripped in the forest and used these to break my fall. I'm not good in rural areas. And to answer your question, we didn't spend much time in the cottage at all. Even if we were so inclined to start pilfering, there wasn't anything that we would want to steal." In my mind I was listing the chest, the lighter fluid and matches as being commandeered for a public service.

"Did you see anybody suspicious while you were there?"

"No, the place was deserted."

Detective Hanlon stared at me and I had to fight not to drop my eyes. I knew this was some kind of dominance play, but what she didn't know was I was not interested in her games.

"Are we finished now?" I was grateful when Conall interrupted. "We were just on our way to breakfast."

"We're done for now," Hanlon said as she snapped the notebook shut. "Just remember to be available if I need to speak to you again." She nodded in Conall's direction and then left, slamming the door behind her.

26

To say Conall and I garnered some attention when we walked into the diner was an understatement. All conversation stopped as Conall directed me to a booth in the middle of the dining area. I slid in across from him, conscious of all eyes being on us.

"Maybe this wasn't such a good idea," I muttered.

Conall captured my hand. "They're going to have to get used to us sooner or later."

I was relieved when the waitress came up to the table to get our order. This seemed to be the signal for everyone to return to their own conversations, although there was no missing the furtive looks sent in our direction.

I'd seen the waitress before, and she'd been friendly with me then. Today she looked at me with undisguised hostility and the expression didn't change the entire time she took our order. When she walked away, I looked around the diner and noticed that quite a few of the women were glaring at me with the same animosity.

"You know, I think I've been patient about the whole town full of ex-girlfriends thing," I mused quietly. "But I've got to tell you, the jealousy vibe that keeps hitting me is getting old really fast."

Conall swiped a hand across his face. "I made a lot of mistakes when I was younger. I wish I could change them, but I can't. Is it going to cause a problem?"

"It's going to make my life difficult for a while." I looked over at the kitchen. "I'm a bit concerned that my food is going to be messed with."

Conall smiled. "You don't have to be worried about that. There's a standard spell on eating establishments that means that any tampering of the food causes the whole thing to decay within five seconds. There is no way to hide doing something like that."

That was a relief. There was something else I noticed. "There seem to be some men looking at me in the same way. Why is that?"

Conall sighed as he leaned back. "How much do you know about werewolf and witch history?"

I chose my words carefully knowing that without a spell stone to hide our conversation, there was every chance that any number of paranormals with enhanced hearing was listening in on us. "I was brought up by a normal mother. History of paranormals was not a subject she knew well."

"There was a time in history when witches enslaved werewolves to do their bidding. It took generations for werewolves to break free of that enslavement. It's a pretty ugly time in both our histories, but the legends are still there, as is the prejudice. Witches feel like one of their own getting seriously involved with a werewolf is a step down, and were-wolves think that a pairing with a witch is a betrayal of the struggles of our ancestors."

I frowned in confusion. "But I thought there was no problem with witches and werewolves dating. In fact, when I first got here, I was warned against getting involved with a werewolf."

"Dating is considered fine, hooking up is considered fine. A lifetime commitment is when the old prejudices start rearing their ugly head."

I shook my head. "So, let me get this straight, not only do I have all your old girlfriends to worry about, but I also have to contend with the werewolf clan not approving of us being together."

Conall looked up as the diner door opened and grimaced when a group of men walked in. "That doesn't even begin to explain how much the alpha family is against this pairing."

I twisted around and saw Aidan Tolan enter the diner, followed by four men who all bore a resemblance to the man sitting across from me. I recognized Conall's brothers, Eamon and Brian. Eamon gave me a concerned nod and Brian sneered in my direction.

I saw the moment Conall's father located us and pure hatred flashed across his face. I just wasn't sure whether it was aimed at me or his son. It looked like I was going to find out when he changed direction and headed straight for us.

Conall straightened up and a stoic look settled across his face. It was so different to the smiling and flirty man that I had been enjoying this morning that I instantly realized that this was the way Conall had learned to deal with his family. The group of men stopped at our booth and you could almost hear everyone in the diner collectively drawing in their breath, waiting to see what would happen next.

"Boy," Aidan growled. "I'm surprised to see you in that uniform."

"I'm still the sheriff," Conall said simply.

Aidan grunted and swung his attention to me. "So, this is to be my new daughter-in-law." He scrutinized me like I was a bug. "How…disappointing."

Conall growled from across the table and I could almost see the hackles on every werewolf in the place rise. I plastered a ridiculous fake smile on my face and grabbed both of Conall's hands across the table, pressing down as if I had a chance of controlling him. I knew his father was baiting him, but I also knew that his father had no idea what it would unleash if he pushed Conall too far. I'd seen it and I wasn't keen to see it explode all over the diner.

Aidan Tolan glared at me and then a small smile danced across his lips. Between one second and the next the atmosphere in the diner changed. It became oppressive as if there was something weighing down on everyone. Heads dipped all around me and when I looked at Aidan, I could see that he was concentrating. In seconds the entire diner seemed to have fallen under whatever power Aidan was using. Some people were simply bowing their heads in deference to the alpha while others had fallen to their knees. I glanced at Conall and saw that he was sitting straight, his head wasn't moving, and his gaze was not leaving his father's face. I turned back to find Aidan focusing in my direction and I stared back at him, making sure my head did not move one bit. The smile on the alpha's face faded as he realized the two people he had hoped to humiliate were the only two who seemed to be immune to his power. Suddenly the oppressive atmosphere dropped, and people started rising from their positions.

"This pairing is an abomination," snapped Conall's father and he stalked out of the diner with the rest of the family following.

I looked around to find that after that display there was no longer just hostility in people's eyes. There was fear.

"What just happened?" I asked as I let go of Conall's hands, confident that he had control of his berserker side.

"I'm not entirely sure," Conall said as he watched me carefully.

At that moment our breakfast arrived, and we ate silently for a while.

"Why did everybody show deference like that?" I asked. "I could understand the werewolf clan doing it, but there are other races in here as well and some of them dropped to the floor."

Conall wiped his mouth with a napkin. "It's the one piece of magic that werewolves have. The alpha is able to force dominance. If he uses the power, it causes everybody to bend to his will."

"You didn't," I pointed out.

"I've never been affected by it," Conall said quietly. "When I was a child, I would pretend just so I would fit in. As an adult I no longer feel the need to be something I'm not. I think the fact that I'm a berserker has something to do with it."

"I guess that makes sense," I replied as I finished off my breakfast.

"I think the more interesting question would be why you weren't affected by it."

I shrugged. "Maybe it's because I'm Flora's niece. I've got the feeling that it wouldn't work on her."

"You would be correct," Conall agreed. "But Flora is the head of the coven. She has enough power in her own right to counter Aidan's ability. The same could be said of all the clan leaders. Other than them, there would be very few people in this town who would be able to withstand a full dominance play, and make no mistake, Aidan put everything into trying to get you to kneel in front of him." Conall paused, his eyes searching mine. "I truly don't understand why it didn't work on you."

"I have no idea," I murmured, a part of me panicking at

the suspicion in Conall's eyes. The last thing I wanted was for him to work out that I may be more powerful than anyone was expecting. I glanced around the room, suddenly feeling closed in and panicked.

"Are you okay?" Conall's concern shone through his eyes.

"I have to admit, I've had better first dates." I gave him a small smile. "Of course, I've also had worse ones."

"I'll try to make sure the next one is an improvement," he murmured.

I looked up as someone new entered into the diner. It was Tilda and she didn't look happy. I smiled at her only to have her walk right past our table and not acknowledge me. Looked like she was still unhappy about being told to leave the cottage. She settled into a booth at the back of the diner.

I looked over at Conall apologetically. "Sorry to bring the date to a close, but I think I need to do some damage control."

Conall smiled. "I don't think you have to worry. Tilda has a tendency to lose her temper quickly, but she forgives pretty easily."

"I hope so," I breathed.

He put his hand over mine as I pulled myself out of the booth. "What are you doing today."

"Why?" I asked, suspiciously.

Conall laughed. "Nothing nefarious. I'm just a little concerned. You have a tendency to get yourself into unfortunate situations."

He had a point. "There's no need to worry. I'm working in the library today. I have no intention of doing anything other than that."

He stood up next to me and kissed me on the forehead.

I frowned. "Why are you kissing me there?" It seemed a little tame considering what our relationship was supposed to be.

I looked up and was almost scorched by the heat in his eyes. "Remember, I'm trying to be sensitive to your need to take things slowly. Trust me, if I was to kiss you properly, we'd be giving everyone a show they might not be ready for."

I swallowed nervously. "Good point." I gave him a quick peck on the cheek. "Be careful."

He laughed and strode off. I watched him as he left the diner. Agnes was right. He did fill that uniform out nicely.

I took a deep breath and headed for the back of the diner. Without waiting for Tilda to object I sat opposite her and held out my hand. "We need the cone of silence stone."

After a couple of seconds Tilda brought it out and placed it in the center of the table. "You know, that's not its name."

"I don't care. That's what I think it should be called." I tapped it a couple of times. "Is it on?"

I could see that Tilda was struggling not to laugh. "It's on. What did you want?"

I clasped both hands in front of me and took on a penitent posture. "I'm sorry that you were ordered away from the cottage yesterday. You should have been able to stay as you were the one who discovered it. The situation sucked." I took in a breath. "I hope you can forgive me."

"A little over the top, don't you think?" Tilda asked dryly.

I smiled. "If you want, I can throw myself at your feet and beg forgiveness."

"Considering you didn't do that for Aidan's dominance play, it would certainly up my standing in the community."

My mouth dropped open. "How did you know about that? It literally only just happened."

Tilda waved her hand in the air. "The gossip in this town is otherworldly, and you and Conall staring down the alpha of the werewolf pack when he was trying to pull a power spell is the number one news item. The werewolves are all having panic attacks and the rest of the clans are laughing at him. If he hadn't already hated you, that little incident would have sealed it."

That was just great, but I could see we had got distracted. "So, back to the forgiving part of the proceedings."

Tilda rolled her eyes. "Fine, I forgive you."

I gave a small jump in my seat. "Good, now do you want me to tell you what we found in there?"

Tilda nodded. "Of course, I do."

"We found…a mussed-up bed."

Tilda frowned. "A mussed-up bed? Why is that important?"

"It indicates Jeanette was having an affair."

Tilda lifted her shoulders. "Or it indicates the house was being used by some homeless person and it was a complete coincidence that I saw Jeanette in the area."

Here was the tricky part. I couldn't tell Tilda that I knew Jeanette was having an affair thanks to the vision I received from the curse tablet. "I still think Jaxon was right about her having an affair."

Tilda went back to her breakfast. "He probably was. I just think we need to wait for more evidence."

"They probably sent the sheets off for DNA testing."

Tilda dropped her food and wiped her hands. "Well, that's just nauseating." She cocked her head. "Do you think they're any closer to finding out who killed Jeanette?"

"I don't know," I said quietly.

I looked up as the diner door opened. I was surprised to see the three leaders of the Path Coven. Violet and Elspeth were leading a reluctant Ilsa Hocking. She looked pale and drawn. It was exacerbated by the stark black dress she was wearing. Violet and Elspeth shot me a dark look as they walked past. Ilsa barely looked conscious as she was dragged to the back of the diner.

"What are they doing?" I couldn't understand why

anybody would drag a grieving mother out into public so soon after the death of her child.

"The coven is concerned that Ilsa might go into a spiral after what happened. They're trying to keep things as normal for her as they can," Tilda replied.

"I don't understand why they would make her do that, not after what happened to Jeanette."

Tilda shivered even though the diner was warm. "It's creepy, isn't it? Somewhere in this town there is somebody capable of killing Jeanette."

"Not just killing her," I reminded Tilda. "They tore her apart so badly that Conall and Karl weren't able to recognize her, and they've known her for a very long time."

Tilda and I sat in silence.

"She didn't deserve that," Tilda remarked.

I kept quiet. I had seen how horrific the curse was that Jeanette had cast around the cottage. My opinions on what she deserved were probably not appropriate for public consumption. I was not quite as forgiving as Tilda.

*A*fter leaving Tilda at the diner I made my way to the coven library. When Tilda's grandmother had suggested that I take over running the library, I had seen it as an opportunity to learn more about the world that I now found myself in. In truth, it had become more of a hunt to find the books on dark magic that the previous librarian had been illegally saving from destruction. As much as it pained me to see knowledge lost in this way, I was beginning to see that some of these books were little more than weapons that could have nightmarish consequences in the wrong hands.

I unlocked the front door and shivered at the coolness of the cave the library had been built in. It didn't take long for me to start cataloging books. Despite Tilda's insistence that the coven would not accept a computerized system, I had brought my laptop along and started creating a rudimentary database. Even if the coven wasn't happy about it, the technology would make my life easier. Before long I was engrossed in my task and fascinated by the age of some of the books I was going through.

I jumped when my phone started ringing, breaking through the silence. Annoyed at the distraction, I answered it. Before I could speak the caller started talking.

"Where are you?"

I frowned at the unfamiliar voice. "Who is this?"

"It's Agnes, I've had a prophecy. You need to listen to me and do exactly what I say."

This was not the shy young woman who had got drunk on our girl's night out and laughed at the stupid jokes we were telling. This voice vibrated with the power of the Seer. Even over the phone I could tell that whatever was going to happen next was not going to be good.

"You are in danger. Jeanette's killer is coming after you and he is going to kill you. You need to get to the sheriff immediately. He's the only one who can protect you."

I didn't need to be told twice. "I'm leaving the library now," I said as I grabbed my bag and headed for the door.

"Hurry," Agnes said urgently, and I could hear her voice thickening with tears. "He wants to hurt you and he's going to enjoy it."

Even while my heart clenched with fear, I could also feel sympathy for the woman who had obviously just seen something traumatic. I hoped she would never give me details about what she saw.

"Who is it?" I asked urgently as I reached my car and started to unlock it.

"It's…"

I was slammed against the car and dropped the phone.

"Surprised?"

My heart clenched at the whisper in my ear. I didn't need Agnes's prophecy to tell me that this man wanted to see me die painfully. My phone was on the ground and I hoped that Agnes could hear what was going on. I struggled against the iron grip I was held in, but it was no use. I only had one option. I screamed, as loudly and as long as I could, and only stopped when I felt the heavy blow on the back of my head and fell to the ground. I looked up and, through the darkness that seemed to be encroaching, I saw Brian Tolan's face glaring down at me.

"There's no point screaming. Nobody's going to get to you in time. You are going to pay for ruining everything," he snarled.

Despite fighting to stay awake, there was a part of me that was grateful when the blackness overtook me. Agnes was right, Brian wanted to hurt me.

NOT FOR THE first time I drifted back to consciousness after being kidnapped. I had a feeling this time was going to be a whole lot worse than the last. I forced my eyes open and discovered that I was in the cottage on Henrietta's property. Despite my fears, I wasn't restrained. I pushed myself up and found Brian sitting on a chair, staring at me.

I sat with my back against the wall and waited to see what happened next. Frankly, I was stunned that I was still alive. When I'd seen his face, contorted with hate, I was sure that would be the last thing I saw on this earth.

"Where is it?"

"Where is what?" I croaked.

"The box. I need to know where it is."

I frowned as my sluggish mind tried to keep up. "What box?"

Brian launched himself over to me, grabbed my hair and pulled my head back. I yelped in shock.

"The box that was in here. I need it now." He was yelling

in my face and my mind finally caught up with the situation. The only thing keeping me alive was Brian's belief that I could produce the box I had found in the cottage. The box I had drowned in lighter fluid, set on fire and then scattered the ashes.

I kept silent, terrified that saying the wrong thing would be the last thing I ever said.

He pushed my head back and it slammed against the wall.

"We've got everything contained but if we can't find that box…" He muttered to himself as he walked away.

"What are you going to do with me?" I tried to keep my voice even and calm, despite the panic racing through me.

He was pacing back and forth shaking his head. "You have to die, just like Jeanette had to die." His voice was indifferent, as if telling me the weather forecast.

It looked like I had only one card to play. "If you kill me, you'll never get the box back."

"You're lying," Brian snarled.

I cast my mind back. "It had a symbol on the front. Kind of like a wiggly line crossing a circle." I hadn't paid much attention to the box at the time, the paper inside taking all my attention, but I did remember the top of it.

Brian grabbed my arms and hauled me to my feet. "Where is it?"

"I hid it in the forest near here. I was going to go back for it when everything died down. You will never find it without me."

Sure, I knew I was lying through my teeth, but by this point I figured lying was the only way I would survive long enough to escape the situation I was in.

Brian studied me, a calculated look in his eyes. "You are going to take me to where you hid the box."

"Why should I?" I challenged, trying to project a bravery I didn't feel.

Brian smiled in a way that chilled my soul. "If you don't, I will rip you to pieces right now and drop them on that bench you like so much for my darling little brother to find."

My stomach clenched with fear. "I'll take you to the box."

"*Y*ou do know what Conall is going to do to you, don't you?"

Brian laughed as he dragged me out of the cottage. "There has never been a day when I haven't been able to best my little brother. He's only going to survive long enough to know you died painfully."

In spite of my fear, I was comforted by the surprise Brian was going to get when he discovered what Conall in a full berserker rage would do to him.

He pushed me forward and I started to lead him to the clearing. Thankfully, the track that Flora had taken in the car was easy to follow. I could see Brian getting frustrated with my slow going. With my hands tied together and the dizziness from the blows to my head, I kept stumbling on the uneven ground.

After we had been walking for a while, I could feel his aggression building when he shoved me in the back and I fell forward onto my knees, my hands barely stopping me from going face first into the dirt. Dropping my head, I saw his legs right behind me. In a move that surprised even me, I brought one of my legs forward and then struck back with my foot into his knee. I heard Brian give a cry and fall backwards, his head hitting a rock. Without thinking, I pushed myself up and started running as fast as I could. I only had a slight head start when I heard a sound that chilled me to the bone. A wolf's howl sliced through the still air and I knew what was coming after me. Fear lent me some speed and I used it to put as much distance between me and the monster that was hunting me.

I stumbled when I made it to the clearing and fell to the ground. I whipped around as I heard growling and held back a whimper when I saw what had been chasing me. Brian had changed into his wolf form, and if I thought he was scary as a human, that was nothing to the fear I had now. He was huge, easily bigger than a normal wolf. His fur was a solid gray color which seemed to absorb the light around it. I scrambled back until my hand found a large stick.

"Stay back." I held the stick in front of me in what I was hoping was a threatening manner as I clambered to my feet.

Brian threw back his head and howled. When he lowered it, I could have sworn that he was smiling, drool dripping from his mouth. I swallowed to get rid of the metallic taste of fear in my mouth. Brian started circling me, his pace slow and measured. With each circle, he got closer and closer. I knew he was toying with me. He seemed to be feeding off my terror, enjoying every moment of the hunt. A small part of me wished that I had learned at least some magic, anything that I could use to defend myself. If I thought there was a chance I was going to survive this, I would have promised myself that I was going to throw myself into learning everything about being a witch. I never wanted to feel this powerless again. I straightened my shoulders and gripped the stick tighter. I had no illusions about what was going to happen next, but I was going to go down fighting.

Brian stopped in front of me, his ears erect and his fur bristling. He started to crouch down and I could tell that he was about to pounce. I widened my stance, hoping to absorb some of the impact when he hit me. He waited. I was trapped and we both knew it.

"Stop right there." The commanding voice rang out through the forest.

A sob erupted from me at the appearance of Conall and Eamon Tolan. I didn't know how they'd found me, but I was beyond grateful that they had. Agnes had told me that Conall was the only one that could protect me, and I knew it was true.

Brian swung around to his brother, his moves slow and deliberate.

Conall moved towards him. "Don't do this, Brian. You know it can only end badly for you."

Brian huffed as if he was chuckling. I could understand why. At the moment, the difference between the two of them was laughable. Brian in his wolf form was large and dominated the clearing. Next to him, the sheriff looked like prey. Of course, I was the only one in this clearing who had seen Conall in his berserker form. I had a feeling Brian was going to be in for a shock.

Brian's next move happened so fast it took everyone by surprise. He spun around, crouched and launched himself at me. I brought up my stick but knew it was a pitiful defense against the monster determined to destroy me. There was a cracking sound and then the body that was aimed straight at me got thrown off course as Conall hit him. The two brothers fell to the ground and clambered up facing one another. Conall had changed into his berserker form, halfway between human and animal. Some would call him the true monster in the clearing, but I knew differently. I could see the shock in Brian's eyes as he took in his brother.

"Holy mother of…" Eamon breathed.

I hadn't realized that he had moved his way around the open space and was now standing next to me, his face a combination of wonder and horror.

I flinched as Brian tried to dodge his way around Conall and found himself flung back across the clearing. He jumped up and charged again. Conall was ready and grabbed his front paws, holding him up as if they were both upright. Brian twisted his head around trying desperately to find a vulnerable part of Conall's body to tear at. While Brian was thrashing around, Conall looked as if he wasn't expending any energy at all. That's why it was such a surprise when he struck, his muzzle opening wide and clamping on Brian's neck.

I looked up at Eamon who was riveted by the scene before him. I elbowed him in the side. "Eamon, I need you to untie me."

For the first time Eamon looked down at me, as if remembering my presence. "You've seen this before," he murmured. "There is no other explanation for you being so calm."

"Yes, been there, done that, got the t-shirt. Now please, listen to the person with experience. You need to get these ropes off me immediately."

"I've seen the old legend scrolls," he breathed. "But I never imagined…"

"That it would be quite so horrifying," I snapped. "I know, but you need to untie me now."

I know Conall believed I was the only one who could pull him back from the berserker rage. I wasn't so sure, but if it was, I wanted to be ready, not trussed up in the background.

Eamon pulled a knife from his back pocket and started sawing at the ropes. We both winced at a crunching sound and Brian's agonized yelp. When the ropes fell, I looked over at the battling brothers. Unsurprisingly, Brian was definitely getting the worst of it. Despite his earlier boasting, he wasn't even close to being a match for Conall. Ignoring my personal opinion that Brian deserved every bit of pain he was now feeling, I knew I had to stop this. I stepped forward only to feel Eamon's hands clamp down on my arms. I struggled to pull myself away.

"For the love of the Fates would you stop doing that," he growled through gritted teeth. "If Conall thinks for a moment I am hurting you, he is going to tear me apart too."

"Let me go," I snarled, not letting up. "He's going to kill him."

"Better him than me."

I stopped my futile struggles and spun around, forcing Eamon to step back at my sudden movement. "If he kills his brother, he won't be able to come back from that and it will always haunt him. I can't let that happen."

"I don't see how you can stop it," replied Eamon with sadness in his eyes. "Brian chose his path, and if he wasn't such a bull-headed idiot, he would have known the consequences of touching you."

"Let me stop this," I pleaded.

Eamon looked down at me and pulled his hands away. "I hope I'm not making a huge mistake," he muttered.

I walked slowly towards the two brothers and gasped as Conall threw the bloodied wolf to the ground. His eyes looked crazed and I knew a moment of panic. Glancing quickly at the crumpled wolf on the ground I knew I had to act now, or it would be too late.

"Conall," I called softly.

He spun around and I knew from the swift intake of breath behind me that Eamon could only see the horror before him. The berserker form was ripped from nightmares. It was not beautiful like a wolf would be, and anyone seeing it without knowing the man beneath would be quick to judge him a monster. I knew differently, and it was in that moment that I knew that I would surrender to the Destined Beloved prophecy. This might not have been the man I would have imagined myself with, but I couldn't think of a better man for me. I just had to stop him from killing his brother.

"You need to stop, Conall. He can't hurt me. You saved me." I moved closer and lowered my voice. "Now let me save you."

He stepped towards me, his massive paw-like hand reaching out to touch mine.

"I'm safe and I need you to come back to me. We can't go on that second date with you looking like this," I joked as I reached up and touched his jaw. He tilted his head and leaned into my hand. Once again, I heard the cracking and felt the contortions of his body against mine, the two of us were bathed in a light so intense I had to close my eyes. I heard a grunt and Conall fell against me.

My knees almost buckled under his weight. "Woah, Sheriff, I'm going to need you to lean back a bit." He instantly rocked back on his feet. I looked up and found his eyes staring at me intently.

"Mine," he growled, and crushed his mouth to mine, his kiss desperate as if I was the one thing in the world that made sense to him, and maybe I was.

I allowed myself a moment to sink into his kiss, but I knew we couldn't stay. I pulled back and gasped as his hold on me tightened. "We have to get Brian to a doctor."

He wasn't listening. Conall looked at me and it was as if he saw me for the first time. He lifted his hand to my head which was pounding. "He hurt you." His voice was guttural, and I knew he was close to giving into the berserker rage again.

"If we're going to save him, we have to do it now," Eamon

said from where he was kneeling next to Brian's broken body.

Conall stayed motionless as if undecided.

"Please, he's your brother."

My words seemed to spur him into action. "Fine. Eamon, you grab Brian. We'll take him to the Doc's place. See if there is anything that can be done." Conall gathered his tattered clothes around him and turned to me. "Can you make it to the car, or do you need me to carry you?"

As much as I liked the idea of not having to do more walking, I knew it would be quicker if I kept going under my own steam. "I'm fine. Let's get this done."

I was grateful to find that Conall's truck was close to the clearing. I was also a little surprised.

"How did you know where I was?"

Conall smiled ruefully as he helped Eamon load an unconscious Brian onto the truck bed. "Seems I found one of the benefits of being part of a Destined Beloved prophecy. It's like I have an internal GPS that is locked onto wherever you are. Once I got the hang of it, I headed straight for you."

I wasn't sure how I felt about that.

"I won't use it unless necessary," he promised.

"Make sure you don't."

I turned my back on him as he quickly stripped out of the destroyed remains of his uniform and threw on some clothes he'd pulled out of the back of his truck.

"We'd better get a move on," called Eamon from his position tending the wounded Brian. "I don't know how much longer he's going to last."

Conall and I got in the truck and sped to the medical clinic where we were met by Dr Collias and Deputy Iversen who Conall had contacted while we were on the road.

The four men wrangled the still unconscious werewolf

into the clinic where Dr Collias and his assistant started working on him.

"Did someone want to explain what happened here?" Karl asked as we stood in the waiting room.

"Brian kidnapped me and was going to kill me. Conall stopped him." I'd given the sheriff as many details as I could on the way to the clinic, and my head was hurting too much to go into it again. I touched the back of my skull and felt the stickiness of my blood there. I looked at my hand and felt nauseous, not sure whether it was the sight of my blood or something else that was causing me to feel sick.

"Do you need the doctor to see you?" I could tell Karl was concerned and I wanted to tell him that I thought that might be a good idea, but I was having trouble saying the words. The pain in my head was growing worse and I kept feeling like someone was dimming the lights in the room. I could see Conall was talking to me, but I couldn't make out what he was saying. Finally, I felt myself slipping and the pain blissfully stopped.

*O*nce again, I found myself fighting my way to consciousness in an unfamiliar setting. I was surprised when the first thing I saw was Tilda's face peering down at me.

"Thank the Fates you're awake."

I raised my head and looked around the room. Disappointment slashed through me when I saw she was the only one there.

"What are you doing here?" I croaked, my hand going to my head, grateful that the incessant pounding had stopped.

"That's a nice greeting since I'm the one doing the bedside vigil in case you woke up before everyone got back."

"Don't get me wrong. I'm thrilled that you're here," I said with possibly a touch too much insincerity. "You're just not the person that I expected to see."

"Oh, I know," Tilda said ruefully. "The Doc said you'd be unconscious for another eight hours. The sheriff is going to be ticked when he finds out that wasn't true. It was the only reason Deputy Iversen was able to drag him and Flora away from here."

I pulled myself up into a seating position. "What happened to me? How long have I been out? Why'd they get dragged away?"

Tilda put up a hand. "In answer to your questions. Do you remember Brian kidnapping you?"

I nodded. I had a feeling I was never going to be able to forget, no matter how much I wanted to.

"Well, seems you got hit on the head a few times and you have concussion. Your head has been glued to stop the bleeding and the coven's medical witches put a spell on you to hurry up the healing." She frowned. "Usually that would have put you out for twelve hours, but you've only been down for about four. That's really weird."

"Where is everybody?" The last thing I needed was Tilda trying to work out why I was weird.

"Everyone's at the town hall. Walker Bay is about to explode, and the people who should be here are the only ones stopping it from happening."

I frowned as I tried to keep up with what Tilda was saying. "Why is the town about to explode? We caught the killer."

"The son of the werewolf alpha kidnapped and tried to murder the niece of the Walker Bay coven leader. He also murdered the daughter of one of the Path coven leaders. It takes a lot for the two covens to unite in this town, but they are today, and they all want blood. There hasn't been this much anger between werewolves and witches in a very long time."

"Did Brian survive?" I asked quietly, not sure which answer I was hoping for.

Tilda nodded. "Werewolves can heal from pretty much anything as long as they get medical attention before they die. He's healed enough to be sitting in a jail cell contemplating how bleak his future is going to be. For the first time in his life, his father's influence is not going to help him one little bit."

I flung back the bed covers and swung my legs over the side of the bed, surprised at how high it seemed to be from the floor. I paused to see if the dizziness and nausea would come back. When it didn't, I dropped to my feet.

"What are you doing?" Tilda exclaimed as she rushed to the other side of the bed to grab me by the arms.

"We're going to the meeting," I replied. "I want to see what happens."

"Are you out of your mind? The sheriff and Flora would kill me if you left this bed, and they are two people who have considerable influence over whether I continue having a happy life."

"C'mon," I wheedled. "You can't tell me that you aren't a little annoyed that you're having to stay here with me and miss everything."

I could tell by Tilda's expression that I was right.

"You can take me to the meeting. We'll stay out of sight. With any luck they won't even know we're there."

Tilda rolled her eyes at the utter impossibility of my plan. "Fine, but if either of them sees us, I am shoving you in their path and making a run for it."

I reached over to grab my clothes. "Sounds like a plan."

Despite my admittedly optimistic hope that nobody would notice us as we made our way into the Town Hall, we'd only made it three steps inside the building when we were accosted by an angry deputy.

"Are you insane?" Karl hissed at Tilda. "She's supposed to be unconscious."

"Well, I'm not," I interrupted. "This affects me more than anyone. I should know what's going on."

I could see that Karl wanted to argue. I could also see that there wasn't much he could do about it.

"Fine, just stay away from the sheriff and your aunt," he growled.

I saluted smartly. "Already part of the plan."

"Man, you are a lot of work," he muttered as he walked away.

I looked around the meeting. The Council was up on the stage again, but there was no pretense of anyone getting along. Aidan and Flora were shaping up to each other. Normally it would have looked ridiculous, the tall broad man towering over the small gray-haired woman, but everyone knew that Flora wasn't as defenseless as she looked. There were small groups everywhere. Discussions happening with some, arguments with others. Conall and his deputies seemed to be everywhere, ensuring that the arguments didn't get out of hand. To one side was Ilsa Hocking, surrounded by members of her coven. She was dressed in stark black and seemed to have aged years in the last few days. The glare she had fixed on Aidan Tolan was one full of hate.

Tilda pointed to a couple of seats at the back, conveniently right behind a group of ogres. "Nobody should be able to see us there," she said.

I nodded and we slid into the seats. Tilda sat on the aisle in the hope her body would shield me from anyone's eyes. I had to give her points for trying. Unfortunately, I had a bad feeling it wouldn't work for long.

I knew the moment Conall realized I was in the room. I saw him look up from the conversation he was having, as if something had caught his attention and he wasn't entirely sure what. He looked around and, before long, his gaze locked on to where we were sitting, hunched behind the ogres. I sighed heavily. I really wasn't impressed with the fact that I seemed to have a locator beacon on me that he could lock on target at any time.

"I think you might want to start running," I murmured to Tilda.

"Why?" She looked around the ogre in front of her and groaned before clambering over me, so I now had the seat closest to the aisle.

"That was graceful," I pointed out breathlessly after copping her knee to my ribs during her mad scramble.

"We all know what happened to Brian. The new rule in town is nobody gets between you and that man. That includes me."

It didn't take long for the sheriff to ignore everyone who wanted his attention and make his way to my side. "What is she doing here?" Conall growled as he reached for me and pulled me into his arms.

"She insisted," Tilda said helplessly. "She may not act like it, but she's got a stubborn streak. Consider yourself warned."

"I'm fine," I interrupted.

"You're supposed to be unconscious."

I lifted my head from where he'd clamped it against his chest. "Sorry to disappoint you, but whatever the doctor and the healers did made me feel a lot better. I need to be here. I need to know why this happened."

Conall kissed my forehead. "We're not going to find that out here. This is just different groups posturing and yelling at each other. All we're doing here is trying to ensure the town doesn't tear itself apart."

I noticed for the first time the level of noise in the Town Hall had lessened considerably. I looked up and found a lot of people staring in our direction.

It didn't take long for the Council to notice what was happening on the floor.

"What is she doing here?' Aidan Tolan thundered.

I felt Conall's body tense, but before he could do anything Flora slammed her hand on the table.

"She is my niece and the aggrieved party. She has every right to be here. You should be on your knees begging her forgiveness for what your son did to her."

I didn't see that happening anytime soon, although I could see many people in the audience appreciated the fantasy.

"My son is being unjustly accused."

There was no way I was going to let him get away with such a blatant untruth. "Your son attacked me. He told me that he was going to kill me in the same way he killed Jeanette. He was going to tear my body to pieces and leave them in the park for Sheriff Tolan to find."

"I have not yet concluded my investigation."

I closed my eyes as Detective Hanlon joined the conversation. I hadn't noticed her standing near the front.

"And you won't be," stated Conall. "I voluntarily stood aside when certain members of the community intimated I could be involved with Jeanette Hocking's murder. I am no longer standing aside. This investigation was hijacked by special interest groups from the start. That is not happening anymore. I am sheriff of this town. If anyone wants to challenge that, I welcome it. Until then, I will be the one who investigates all crimes in Walker Bay, starting with this one."

I could see the fear on a lot of the faces, especially the werewolves. It seemed that Brian's crushing defeat at the hands of his runt brother had sent panic through the clan.

Aidan glared at us, the hate obvious in his eyes. With a tilt of his head, the entire werewolf clan made their way out of the building, with Detective Hanlon following behind her alpha.

"I'm guessing that was a bad sign," I murmured.

"There's nothing they can do." Conall stroked my arm.

"The evidence against Brian is insurmountable. For the first time in his life, Aidan can't get him out of the mess he's made for himself." He shook his head sadly. "A werewolf attacking witches. Brian's marked for life now. Even if he gets out of prison in the future, the Conclave will never let him go free."

I shivered at Conall's words and the acceptance behind them. In the back of my mind was the thought that if the Conclave ever found out about me, I would suffer the same fate as the man who would have murdered me.

"Sadie."

In my aunt's voice was a wealth of pain. Conall reluctantly let me pull away and Flora threw herself into my arms.

"I should have protected you better," she murmured as she cradled my face, peering into my eyes as if she could see everything that happened to me.

"I'm fine," I said. "Conall protected me."

At that moment the main door to the town hall opened and slammed shut.

"Don't you ever do that to me again."

Before I knew it, Flora was moved aside and Agnes had taken her place. Except in her case she was sobbing against my chest. I was surprised as the building cleared out at the sight of the Seer showing some honest emotion.

"You have no idea how horrible it was," she whispered, the trauma evident in her voice.

"I'm sorry you saw that." I held her a bit longer until Flora pulled her off me and led her away.

"Will she be okay?" I asked worriedly.

Tilda put her hand on my arm. "It's the burden of the Seer. Usually, I think it's not so bad because she doesn't really know the people she has visions about. You were different. It might take her a while to get over this one. Flora will take care of her."

"What happens now?" I asked.

Conall smiled at me. "Now, Tilda will take you home. I go back to work. Somebody needs to speak to Brian and find out why he would do something like this."

"You'll let me know what happened?" I asked.

He pulled me into his arms and brushed his lips over mine. "Tomorrow I will tell you everything."

I stepped away from him and followed Tilda out the building. Before we got to the car I felt a touch on my arm. I turned around and found Ilsa Hocking and Myra Hallybread standing there. Ilsa grasped my hands and closed her eyes as if concentrating. After a couple of seconds, she opened them, and a frown crossed her features.

"Thank you for bringing my baby's killer to justice," she murmured.

"The sheriff is the one who brought him in," I protested.

She didn't disagree with me, and I pulled my hands away and put them behind my back.

"Did he say anything about Jeanette?" Myra asked urgently.

I shook my head slowly. "Not much, just that he killed her."

My answer seemed to satisfy them because they walked away without a word.

"That was weird," Tilda commented when the two women were out of hearing range.

I nodded. I was glad I wasn't the only one who thought so.

"*You* only barely survived today. Why are you risking your life sitting up here?"

I shouldn't have been surprised to see Flora climbing the rickety steps up to my deck on the garage roof.

"The stars are beautiful and I'm having a bit of trouble getting to sleep."

Flora picked her way carefully across the rotting wood and sat down next to me.

After a few minutes of silence, she laid her head on my shoulder. "I'm sorry I wasn't there for you today," she said quietly.

I patted her hand. "It all worked out in the end. How's Agnes doing?"

"She's traumatized. It's the reason the Seer is kept separate from everybody. It's far easier to have a prophecy that bad when there's no emotional investment. Unfortunately, she seems pretty emotionally invested in you and Tilda."

I could hear the reproving tone in Flora's voice, but I couldn't bring myself to feel sorry for my newfound friendship with Agnes, especially not today.

"Maybe because we're the first people to treat her like she's more than just the Seer."

Flora didn't reply. I didn't know whether that was because she agreed or whether she recognized that nothing she said was going to change my mind.

"I need to tell you something," I said quietly.

Flora instantly came alert.

I stared out at the darkness. "The only reason Brian didn't kill me immediately was because he wanted the box."

"The one with..."

"Yes. He kept saying that he had to have the box." I licked my lips that had suddenly gone dry. "I've been thinking about something."

"What is it?"

I lowered my voice, a part of me paranoid that someone would hear us. "When I destroyed the tablet, I could feel Jeanette's essence on it. She definitely cast the curse, but..."

"But what?"

"I don't think she wrote the curse. I felt something or someone else around the tablet and the piece of paper."

Flora frowned. "You don't think she found them in a book and used them?"

I shook my head. "They didn't feel old. They felt new like they were at the peak of their strength."

"You think we have someone else who is writing curses?" I could hear the dismay in her voice.

"And willing to sell or give them to other witches.," I concluded.

"I hope you're wrong," Flora said fervently.

"So do I," I agreed.

After Flora left, I went back in my bedroom. After a couple of minutes of looking through the glass doors out to the deck, I grabbed a chair and tucked it under the door-knobs. I knew Flora had put wards around the house, but this day had shaken my confidence. I figured a little extra security wasn't going to hurt anyone, and it might help me sleep. I curled up in my bed, holding my body tightly as the fear I had been holding onto so tightly was finally able to be let go. I sobbed into my pillow as my mind replayed every moment from Agnes's phone call to getting Brian to the clinic. No matter what I did, the tears kept coming until the exhaustion overtook me.

I WOKE up slowly to a feeling that I wasn't alone. I turned over and saw the shadow in the doorway. Considering how the day had been, you would have thought that I would panic at a strange person in my house, but I instinctively knew who it was.

"You really need to stop this breaking and entering habit, Sheriff. I don't think it's something you want coming up at your next election."

"I don't think anyone's going to stop me. It seems that after almost killing my brother, I've gone from being the laughingstock of the werewolf clan to the most dangerous member of the community. It would be funny if it wasn't all so tragic."

"My aunt could probably give you a run for your money, so I wouldn't get so comfortable taking liberties if I was you."

Conall chuckled. "Thank you. I needed something to laugh about today."

I pulled myself up and sat against the headboard. "What did he say?"

He walked towards the bed and sat on the end. "He admitted to killing Jeanette. We found some fur on the body and the DNA matched his."

"You can get DNA from werewolf fur?" That sounded

amazing and not like any crime show episode I had ever seen.

Conall nodded. "Yep, those samples were sent off before Hanlon got on the scene. It seems all evidence samples that were sent off after she arrived were contaminated."

"So, that fur is the only evidence you have?"

"That, your eyewitness testimony and a full confession to the murder of both Jeanette Hocking and Jaxon McDonald."

"I can't believe he confessed." That didn't sound like the Brian Tolan I had learned to loathe. "Did he say why he did it?" I queried.

Conall gave a short laugh. "He was quite forthcoming. He and Jeanette were having an affair and she was pushing him to formalize it. With werewolves and witches not being the ideal pairing for the alpha family, when she threatened to force his hand by telling his far more appropriate werewolf girlfriend, he snapped. Jaxon had to die because there was a possibility he'd worked out who his girlfriend had been cheating on him with. He decided to kill you to cover his tracks and to throw me off the trail."

"He believed that killing me was going to destroy you," I murmured. "He enjoyed telling me how he'd leave my body in pieces for you to find. He said I had to die." I looked more carefully at Conall. "You don't believe him, do you?"

"I believe he killed her and would have killed you."

"But you don't believe the reason he's giving you."

Conall shook his head. "Brian's a bully with a short fuse, but there is no reason for him to have killed Jeanette or you. If he had just been having an affair with Jeanette, there would have been no shame in him admitting to a fling and tossing her aside. Most of the clan would have understood perfectly and it wouldn't have even been a blip on their radar. He was definitely taking orders from somebody."

"Do you have any idea who?" I asked.

Conall looked down at me. "I've got a pretty good theory."

I had a bad feeling I knew where this was going. "Jaxon said before he died that Jeanette would have been cheating on him with somebody who wasn't available and who could give her something she didn't already have."

"My father," Conall said softly. "There had been rumors that he was involved with somebody new, but nobody knew or was willing to admit they knew who it was. Jeanette was my father's type completely, but if she was looking for more than a clandestine affair, she was going to be sorely disappointed. There is no way the alpha of the werewolf clan would have a witch partner. With the history of witches enslaving werewolves, it's a very sensitive area. No werewolf who wants to keep their ranking in the hierarchy would ever get seriously involved with a witch. If Jeanette was threatening to make a relationship with him public, she would have become a liability. She may have also known about some of his dealings that he wanted to keep quiet. There are any number of reasons why my father wanted to get rid of Jeanette. One word to Brian and that problem would be taken care of. Killing you as well would have the added benefit of hurting me in addition to muddying the suspect pool."

"Do you really think that's what happened?" I asked.

Conall nodded.

"Is there any way you can prove any of it?"

Conall shook his head. "Not unless Brian turns on his father."

"Any chance of that?"

Conall shook his head again. "Brian has a lot of distasteful qualities, but there is one person in this world that he is totally loyal to, and that is the alpha. He will never confess to killing somebody on our father's orders. He would rather spend the rest of his life in prison than disappoint Aidan Tolan."

"Do you have anything else other than your gut instinct to support this theory?"

Conall grimaced. "The DNA from the sheets in the cottage came back."

"Whose was it?" I could tell from the look on his face that I really didn't want to know the results.

"There were three separate DNA profiles on those sheets. Jeanette's, Brian's, and my father's."

I was right. I could have lived without that knowledge. "Do you think that they…?"

Conall shook his head, the distaste obvious. "I think they were both having an affair with her, but I would guess, knowing both men, that they only just found out about each other. It would have been one of the main reasons to kill her. Aidan could never stand the shame of sharing a mistress with one of his sons."

I was going to try to purge the mental image that I now had stuck in my head. "That's proof, why can't you use it?"

Conall grimaced. "I took that sample while I was not supposed to be working the case. I sent it to a private lab rather than the Paranormal Crime Lab, and I may have previously obtained samples of my father's DNA in a way that may not stand up in court."

"So, we have proof that your father may have been involved somehow, but nothing we can use." That was disheartening, because I had a feeling that Aidan Tolan was going to do everything in his power to destroy his son. I frowned as Conall's words filtered through. "Why do you have samples of your father's DNA?"

Conall rubbed his hand over his face. "I'm sure you've heard the rumor that I may not be Aidan Tolan's son."

I nodded. "I thought that was all just idle gossip."

Conall laid back on the bed and looked up at me. "About a year ago I obtained some of Aidan's DNA to do a paternity test."

"What did it say?"

Conall stretched his arm out and put his hand on my leg. "I don't know. I've got the envelope at home, but I never looked at it."

"Why ever not?"

Conall smiled ruefully. "Because I have no idea which outcome I'll be happier with."

I kind of understood that. I looked down and saw that his eyes were drooping. "You need to get some sleep. I'll set up the couch for you." I went to get out of the bed but felt his hand tighten on my leg.

"Can I sleep here tonight?" He smiled at the momentary look of panic on my face. "I promise I won't take liberties. I just need to feel you close, to know that I wasn't too late."

"Okay," I whispered as I settled back in the bed.

I looked at my hands while Conall removed his uniform and slid into the bed next to me. I laid down and shivered as he took me in his arms, the heat of his body warming me against any residual fears I had.

"What are you doing here, Conall?" I asked as I lay against him.

He stroked his hand down my arm. "I finished interrogating Brian and I was headed home when I just automatically came here. It seems that when my instincts take over, you're my home now."

"Is this real?" I whispered, almost afraid of the answer.

He kissed me softly, his thumb stroking my cheek. "As real as it gets. I'm yours now, and I always will be."

ABOUT THE AUTHOR

Leonie Gant started her writing career at the age of ten when she stuffed notes in her pencil case full of ideas for mysteries that Nancy Drew and the Hardy Boys should really have been solving. After years of watching mysteries play out in her head she decided that writing them down was the best way to deal with them.

In her life away from writing, she is a voracious reader with not nearly enough time to make her way through all the books she wants to read. She enjoys bushwalking, sewing and chocolate, possibly not in that order. She also believes in the value of trying new things, walking in the rain, and enjoying every moment.

To find out more about Leonie Gant and her books

www.leoniegant.com

ALSO BY LEONIE GANT

Discover other titles by Leonie Gant

The Harstone Legacy

Curse the Dark

Curse the Soul

Curse the Heart

Curse the Past

Not in Hollywood

Not Famous in Hollywood

Not Happily Married in Hollywood

Not Talented in Hollywood

Not Wanted in Hollywood

Not Suspicious in Hollywood

Not Forgotten in Hollywood

www.ingramcontent.com/pod-product-compliance
Lightning Source LLC
Chambersburg PA
CBHW022058170626
46808CB00002B/493